THE ANGEL

For months, Scotland Yard was interested in the mysterious Angela Kesson, who they dubbed 'the Angel', with her striking beauty. Her male acquaintances had dubious reputations. And in every instance, at the start of each relationship, their homes were burgled and money and valuables stolen. Though unemployed, she lived in an expensive flat, but there was insufficient proof for an arrest. However when her latest escort's home was burgled — he had been murdered, his head crushed like an eggshell . . .

Books by Gerald Verner
in the Linford Mystery Library:

GERALD VERNER

THE ANGEL

Complete and Unabridged

LINFORD
Leicester

First published in Great Britain

First Linford Edition
published 2012

British Library CIP Data

Verner, Gerald.
   The Angel. - - (Linford mystery library)
   1. Detective and mystery stories.
   2. Large type books.
   I. Title II. Series
   823.9′12–dc23

   ISBN 978–1–4448–1259–6

Published by
F. A. Thorpe (Publishing)
Anstey, Leicestershire

Set by Words & Graphics Ltd.
Anstey, Leicestershire
Printed and bound in Great Britain by
T. J. International Ltd., Padstow, Cornwall

This book is printed on acid-free paper

1

The Girl in the Box

Jimmy Holland patted the ends of his tie into position, examined the result in the mirror over the dressing table with a critical eye, and gave a nod of satisfaction.

He was tall and dark, with the build of an athlete, and the grey eyes that looked back at him held a humorous twinkle in their depths.

Why, with a yearly income running into five figures, he should ever have chosen to join the Metropolitan Police Force, was a constant source of wonder to those who knew him slightly; less of a mystery to his intimate friends who understood something of the urge which had prompted this step.

His father, a dignified and respected member of the Cabinet, was horrified when Jimmy had calmly announced his intention, for he had visions of an under-secretaryship and a brilliant politi-cal career for his only son.

'You — you can't become a — a common policeman!' he expostulated, aghast at the bare idea. 'It's — it's ridiculous and absurd!'

'It's neither ridiculous nor absurd!' retorted his son. 'I not only can, but I have become a 'common policeman', as you call it.'

And to prove it, he turned up the next day in a brand new uniform to meet the scandalised old man as he left the House of Commons after a debate.

Several things contributed to Jimmy Holland's rapid promotion, the greatest of which was a very real interest in his job. Two years after he had joined the force, he was a sergeant, and a year later was transferred to the C.I.D., owing to the clever way in which he had run to earth and arrested Dan Flecker, of dubious memory, when older and more experienced men had failed to find that cold-blooded murderer. He held the rank of detective-inspector, with the imminent prospect of further promotion. Now he dressed to keep his appointment with the Honourable Freddie Babbington, eldest son of Lord Deeping, and one of his oldest friends.

He was pulling on his dinner jacket when his servant entered, a portly man, with the benign appearance of an archbishop. He advanced with great dignity and presented a silver tray.

'Your sherry, sir,' he said, in the low voice of the well-trained servant.

'Thanks, Limpet. Stick it down somewhere,' said Jimmy. 'Have you ordered that taxi?'

Limpet bowed and carefully set the glass down on the corner of the dressing table.

'The taxicab, sir,' he replied, 'will be at the door in exactly three minutes. I presume, sir, that as you are spending the evening with Mr. Babbington, you will be late.'

'I should think it is quite likely,' said Jimmy.

'I have taken the liberty, sir,' continued Limpet tonelessly, 'of ordering a fresh supply of aspirin, which I will leave in a

3

conspicuous position on the dining room table. If you will remember, sir, the last time you spent the evening with Mr. Babbington, you consumed a complete bottle of fruit laxative tablets on your return due to a slight misapprehension, and the result was extremely disconcerting.'

'You talk exactly like an advertisement,' said Jimmy admiringly. 'Now get out and let me finish dressing.'

The imperturbable Limpet bowed and withdrew.

When Jimmy had first taken the flat in Ryder Street, he had rung up an agency for a manservant. None of the several applicants had appealed to him, and a conference at the Yard had forced him to leave before he could interview the last. On his return late in the evening, the door had been opened, to his astonishment, by the dignified Limpet, and Jimmy discovered that instead of engaging a servant, a servant had engaged him.

Limpet had apparently arrived soon after he had left for the conference, persuaded the hall porter to open the door of the flat with his pass key, and immediately taken up his duties.

The outraged Jimmy had at first been extremely annoyed at this high-handed method of obtaining a situation, but his remarks had no effect whatever. And since the man's references were of the highest, he had eventually capitulated. And he had never had cause to regret it. Limpet ran the small flat with a smooth efficiency that amounted to genius, and was in every respect the ideal servant, even though he was more fictional than real.

When Jimmy arrived at the Ritz-Carlton, he saw the huge figure of the Honourable Freddie Babbington waiting in the foyer.

Freddie was a tremendous man. His stature was enormous; his big, red face one huge grin of delight.

'Cheerio! Well met, and what not!' he roared, in a voice that brought every other occupant of the vestibule to startled attention. 'You're two minutes late, but what does that matter? What's a couple of minutes between friends?'

'The same as between anyone else, I presume,' said Jimmy, ruefully rubbing his fingers, which had been almost squashed by the beefy hand of his friend. 'Even if it is your birthday, it doesn't entitle you to assault a police officer of high rank. What's the programme?'

'Food!' boomed Babbington. 'And then a trifle of light amusement. I've got a box at the Mayfair.'

Jimmy grunted disparagingly.

'The sort of entertainment you would choose,' he remarked. 'Legs and lyrics, and neither very good.'

'On a man's birthday,' said the Honourable Freddie, as an obsequious head waiter conducted them to their table, 'legs and lyrics are what the doctor ordered.'

'Oh, well,' said Jimmy resignedly, 'you're paying the bill, so it's up to you to call the tune.'

'It'll do you good,' said his friend. 'Take your mind off policewomen with large feet. Froth and frivolity — that's the keynote of the evening! Frills and fancies and snappy tunes! Wine, women and — damn!'

6

In his excitement he had knocked over the vase of flowers that decorated the table.

Throughout the meal that followed, Freddie babbled continuously, so that Jimmy had little to do but listen and eat the very excellent dishes that were set before him. He continued his ceaseless string of anecdotes and gossip on the way to the theatre, and kept it up even after they had taken their places in the box, which he had reserved.

The orchestra was on the point of beginning the noisy overture which heralded 'Swing High', when Babbington stopped abruptly in the middle of his ceaseless chatter and gripped Jimmy by the arm.

'Look!' he breathed, in what, for Freddie, was a whisper, but which in any other man would have been a normal tone of voice. 'Oh, boy! Just look!'

Jimmy followed the direction of his eyes, and saw that two people had, at that moment, entered the box opposite. One was a rather short, fattish man, with an almost completely bald head and an unpleasant face consisting chiefly of rubbery lips and a fleshy nose.

The other was a girl. She was dressed in white, and was of medium height. Her hair, a gleaming mass of curls, was the colour of sun-kissed honey. Her face, almost a perfect oval, was lovely, with a loveliness that was both warm and ethereal. Her well-shaped head, the slender column of her neck, the creamy whiteness of her arms and shoulders, enhanced by the dark background of the box, was a picture that would have delighted the eye of an artist, and certainly delighted the eye of Freddie Babbington, for he was staring across at the opposite box with an expression on his face that was a cross between a wounded bull and an expiring codfish.

Jimmy chuckled.

'The lady appears,' he said, 'to have struck you all of a heap.'

'Who is she? D'you know?' demanded Freddie, coming out of his trance with a gasp.

'I know her name, if that's what you mean,' answered Jimmy, 'and I'd like to know a lot more about her.'

'By Jove, so would I!' exclaimed his friend. 'Who's that horrible little man with her? Talk about beauty and the beast — '

'The gentleman's name,' said Jimmy, calmly fishing for his cigarette case, 'is Montgomery Webb, and he's not so much of a gentleman, either. As a matter of fact, we've been very interested in Mr. Webb for quite a long time. He has an office in the City and is generally supposed to make his living by dabbling in stocks and shares. But we have an idea that he has more profitable and less legal sidelines — '

'Never mind him,' said Freddie impatiently, as Jimmy paused. 'It's the girl I'm interested in. Who's she?'

Jimmy looked at him thoughtfully.

'She calls herself Angela Kesson,' he answered slowly.

'Why do you say, calls herself?' demanded Babbington.

'Because I'm very doubtful whether that is her real name,' replied Jimmy. 'I'm afraid, Freddie, that any romantic ideas that may have crept into your susceptible young heart are in danger of receiving a rude shock.'

Freddie turned his big face towards him in consternation.

'You don't mean — ' he mumbled. ' — You're not suggesting that — that girl's a crook?'

'I've every reason to believe,' answered Jimmy gravely, 'that she is one of the cleverest thieves in London.'

'What, that beautiful creature?' gasped his friend. 'I don't believe it! What proof have you?'

'That's the trouble,' said Jimmy. 'I haven't any proof. If she knew what I'd said she could sue me for slander. But at the same time everybody at the Yard is of the same opinion.'

Freddie shot another glance in the direction of the opposite box. The girl was talking to her companion, presenting a perfect profile towards him.

'Nobody with a face like that,' he declared, 'could be a crook! You're crazy! Why, she's like an angel!'

'Yes,' said Jimmy. 'That's what they call her, the Angel.'

2

A Midnight Excursion

Mr. Montgomery Webb was enjoying himself. He had fed well, absorbed a large quantity of wine, and been conscious all the time of the envious glances directed at his lovely companion.

She had been the greatest stroke of luck that had ever come Mr. Webb's way; at least, that is how he regarded it in his own mind, being completely unaware how very cleverly the meeting had been arranged.

It was Mr. Webb's habit to leave his office in Cannon Street at exactly one o'clock in order to partake of such refreshments as his physical needs required at an exclusive and expensive restaurant in the vicinity. Descending the stairs on the previous Thursday he had come face to face with a vision of loveliness, which took what little breath he had left completely away. The vision was looking about her rather helplessly, and Mr. Webb, who was never averse to seizing an opportunity, particularly if the opportunity was of the feminine gender, gallantly offered his assistance.

He was rewarded with a slightly pathetic smile, and an inquiry concerning the whereabouts of a firm called Harpole & Simpkins who, according to the fair visitor's information, should have occupied an office in the building that Mr. Webb graced with his presence. Mr. Webb had never heard of the firm in question, which was not surprising since it existed only in the fertile imagination of Miss Angela Kesson. He did his best, however, to find it, and although his efforts were naturally unsuccessful, she appeared so grateful and was so profuse in her thanks that Mr. Webb was emboldened to suggest that she should join him at lunch.

She was charmingly hesitant, but eventually accepted his invitation. She proved a thoroughly agreeable companion, and Mr. Webb made sure before the end of the meal that she would not pass into the vagueness of a memory. They met again for tea on the Saturday and it was then that an appointment was arranged for dinner and a show on the Tuesday.

As the lights dimmed and the curtain rose, he hitched his chair a little nearer to the girl and gave her a sidelong glance from his small, rather pig-like eyes. This time, he thought, he really had struck the 'goods'. There had been many such adventures in his life, but none had come within a thousand miles of this.

The interval came, and Mr. Webb, having for the first time in his life behaved with perfect propriety and as near to a gentleman it was possible for him to get, began to search in his own mind for a good opening which would further his own and not at all gentlemanly ends; curiously enough, his companion's mind was moving on precisely similar lines, though the end in view was not quite the same as Mr. Webb's.

'Enjoying yourself?' he inquired.

Angela nodded

'Yes,' she answered. 'It's a good show,

don't you think?'

'I haven't seen much of it.' Mr. Webb, trying vainly to be subtle, only succeeded in being clumsy. 'I've been too busy looking at you, m'dear.'

'Why? What's the matter with me?' asked Angela innocently.

'Nothing! Nothing!' said Mr. Webb, a little huskily. 'You're perfect! The most beautiful thing I've ever seen!'

'Do you think so?' she murmured softly, and Mr. Webb suddenly felt as if a giant hand had gripped him in the middle of his stomach and turned him inside out.

'Of course I think so,' he breathed. 'Who could possibly see you and not think so?'

He leered at her with what he fondly imagined was a fascinating smile but which reminded Angela of a pig she had once seen contemplating a particularly luscious meal.

'You and I are going to be friends,' he said. 'Good friends, m'dear eh? It was a lucky day for me when you came wandering round Cannon Street.'

'Was it?' said Angela, and wondered

just how long he would continue to think so. 'It's very sweet of you to be so nice to me.'

'Nonsense, m'dear!' said Mr. Webb, patting her knee with a hot hand. 'It's very easy to be nice to you. My niceness is inexhaustible with anyone I really like. I hope this is going to be the beginning of many pleasant little evenings together.'

'I hope so, too,' said Angela untruthfully.

What Mr. Webb might have said in answer to this encouragement is debatable, but happily at that moment the curtain went up on the second half of 'Swing High', and since the girl appeared to be more interested in what was taking place on the stage than his rather ponderous amorous advances, he reluctantly relapsed into silence. But if he refrained from vocally expressing his feelings, he allowed actions to speak even louder than words. His podgy hand slid out stealthily and rested on the top of Angela's.

She made no attempt to pull hers away, and gaining courage from this success

Mr. Webb hitched himself a little nearer. He gave a faint squeeze, and was surprised and delighted to have the gentle pressure returned.

And then he uttered a little sharp exclamation, for something had hurt him.

The girl turned quickly.

'What's the matter?' she asked.

'Something stuck in my hand,' said Mr. Webb.

'Oh, I'm so sorry!' said Angela contritely. 'It must have been my ring.'

'My fault, m'dear,' said Mr. Webb.

'Oh, but I hope I haven't hurt you?' Her face was concerned as she looked at him.

'No! No! It's nothing at all,' he protested. 'I'd go through a lot more than that, m'dear, for the pleasure of holding your hand.'

The latter part of his sentence was slurred and thick. He blinked several times, and licked his thick lips.

'Queer,' he mumbled. 'I feel — It must be the heat — ' His voice trailed away, and he suddenly slumped sideways in his chair against the girl.

She put an arm round him quickly to prevent him falling. The effects of the drug in the ring would pass in a few seconds, and she would have to work quickly.

Rapidly she searched for the platinum chain and pulled it out of his right-hand trouser pocket. From a ring on the end depended half a dozen keys. She examined them swiftly, her level brows drawn together. Choosing a Yale, she slipped it from the ring, and pulling up her dress, thrust it into the top of her stocking.

When Mr. Webb recovered, she was leaning solicitously over him, her beautiful face creased with anxiety.

'Oh!' she said as he sat up dazedly. 'You did frighten me.'

'I must have fainted,' he grunted, rubbing his forehead. 'Stupid of me — '

'Would you like to go?' she asked anxiously. 'Perhaps the air — '

'No, no!' he interrupted. 'I'm quite all right now, m'dear. I'm very sorry to have alarmed you, although it's partly your fault you know.'

She was momentarily startled, but his next words relieved her anxiety.

'I'm not as young as I used to be, and — well, the society of so charming a girl — '

He smiled at her, leaving the sentence unfinished. Inwardly he was a little alarmed, for his doctor had warned him that his heart was not as good as it might be. That his attack had had anything to do with the girl he never suspected, and he was only annoyed with himself that such a thing should have happened in the presence of Angela when he was anxious to appear at his best. But he had no intention of allowing such a trifle to interfere with the plan that had been gradually forming in his mind during the evening.

As they came out of the theatre at the end of the show and the commissionaire went to call his car, he made his suggestion.

'The night is yet young,' he said, as they stood amidst the stream of people in the foyer. 'What d'you say to running up to my place for a bit of supper? It's not far. I live at Hampstead, and the car can take you home.'

Angela, who was perfectly well aware

that he lived at Hampstead, but had other plans, shook her head.

'Not tonight, if you don't mind,' she said. 'I'm feeling very tired. Some other night I'd love to.'

Mr. Webb tried every means in his power to persuade her, but without result.

He dropped her at her flat near Baker Street, after arranging an appointment for the following evening, and was driven home, a contented and complacent man, his mind full of what he fondly believed was a fresh conquest — and completely unaware that there would be no other night so far as he was concerned.

Angela stepped into the lift and was carried up to the third floor, very satisfied too with her night's work, or that part of it that was over. As she entered the tiny vestibule of her flat her maid came out of the kitchen to meet her.

'Well, 'ave a good time?' she greeted nasally.

'Have you ever been to the Zoo, Cordelia?' asked Angela.

Cordelia Smith wrinkled her uptilted nose.

'Can't say as I 'ave, not since I was a nipper,' she answered. 'Why, wot's the Zoo got ter do with it? You ain't been to no Zoo, 'ave yer, miss?'

'I feel rather as if I had,' said Angela. 'I feel as if I'd spent the evening in the reptile-house!'

She passed into her bedroom, followed by the maid, and began rapidly to divest herself of her white satin gown.

'Bring me my old tweeds,' she said. 'And the brown brogues.'

Cordelia's small black eyes widened.

'Why, wot yer goin' to do, miss?' she asked. 'You surely ain't goin' out agin at this time o' night.'

'I am,' said Angela. 'And don't ask questions, Cordelia — do as you're told!'

Cordelia went over to the big wardrobe, sniffing her disapproval.

'You'll get in trouble one of these fine days,' she remarked. 'I've warned yer before, and I'm warning yer agin. And then wot'll 'appen? You'll get nine moons' in the second division, same as my brother Bert.'

'I'm afraid you were never cut out to be

a maid to a burglar,' remarked the Angel, as she pulled off her filmy stockings and drew on a pair of more serviceable woollen ones. 'Or should it be burglaress?'

'It's all the same thing when it comes to the indickment, miss,' said Cordelia pessimistically. 'The 'beak' won't trouble much.'

'We haven't reached that stage yet!' retorted the girl.

'But you never knows when we're goin' to,' answered Cordelia, crossing over and depositing on the bed the tweed costume. 'Whenever you goes off on one of these 'ere jaunts, I waits with me 'eart in me mouth fer some blinkin' 'flatty' ter turn up, sayin' as 'ow you've been pinched in the act. My brother Bert was pinched in the act, an' they locked 'im in a cell and took all 'is clothes away.'

'I hope they'll do nothing so immodest to me,' said Angela.

'You don't know wot them policemen 'ull do,' asserted the maid darkly; 'I wouldn't trust none of 'em. When they pinched my brother Bert — '

'Stop talking and make me a cup of tea,' said Angela. 'Then phone to the garage and ask them to bring my car round.'

Cordelia departed grumbling, and Angela began to dress herself quickly. By the time the maid had brewed the tea she was ready, a neat figure in a worn tweed costume. A plain felt hat covered her shining head, the brim of which was sufficiently large to partially conceal her face.

She carried the tea into the sitting room, and, setting it down on a small table near the fire, went over to a walnut bureau, and, unlocking a drawer, took out a small automatic. Making certain that there was a fresh clip of cartridges in the butt, she dropped it into her pocket.

'And that's the greatest madness of all!' said Cordelia watching this proceeding, her small body eloquent of strong disapproval. 'Don't you know that if you was caught with that thing they'd give yer five years? My brother Bert — '

'Let Brother Bert rest in — Penton-ville,' said the Angel, sipping her tea.

'Have you phoned the garage?'

'Just goin' to,' answered Cordelia. 'I can't do 'alf a dozen things at once, can I?' She picked up the telephone and gave a number. 'Is that you, George? Miss Kesson wants 'er car. Yes, at once. Make it snappy!'

It was two o'clock when the Angel left the flat, her ears full of further pessimistic warnings from Cordelia Smith, and as she sent the little car speeding through the silent streets in the direction of Hampstead, nobody realised more than she did the danger which lay before her.

But the voice of the dead was calling insistently and it had to be obeyed.

3

Murder!

Mr. Montgomery Webb's house was a pretentious establishment standing in its own grounds, and surrounded by a high brick wall, which was broken only by the gates giving admission to the winding drive.

It stood on the edge of the heath, and had been built at the time when the cheap villa was unknown, and the country had not been divided up into residential estates and thereby denuded of its greatest charm.

A clock was chiming the quarter before the hour when the Angel brought her small car to a halt in a deserted side street, and, getting out, set off to cover the rest of the way to her destination on foot.

It was a dark night, with heavy clouds obscuring moon and stars, and there was a hint of rain in the air, but Angela had explored the neighbourhood on a previous occasion in daylight, and the darkness troubled her not at all. Indeed, she welcomed it as an asset, for there was safety in darkness should anything go wrong.

She came to the drive gates and paused, feeling with a gloved hand for the latch. It rose noiselessly under her fingers, and, pushing open the gate a foot or so, she slipped through, closing it gently behind her.

From where she stood she could see nothing of the house itself, for the gravelled approach curved sharply, and a screen of trees hid it from view.

The dark bulk of the house rose before her as she rounded the bend, and she saw, without surprise, that there were no lights in any of the windows. It was hardly likely there would be at such an hour; the servants had long since retired to bed and she had discovered by judicious questions that it was not Montgomery Webb's habit to remain up late. He had himself told her that his invariable custom was to go to bed at twelve and he was the type of man who would not let anything interfere with his normal routine.

She came to the porch and stood in the shadow, feeling in her pocket for the key, which she had stolen during Mr. Webb's short indisposition. There were no bolts or chain to worry about. The lock was a patent one, and Webb relied entirely upon it for the safeguarding of his premises. This she had ascertained during their brief acquaintanceship There was only one risk and that was that he might have discovered his loss. But she discounted this as almost negligible, concluding, and rightly as it happened, that his butler would hear the car arrive and open the door for his master.

Only for a moment did she hesitate at the top of the shallow flight of steps and then, pushing the key into the lock, she twisted it firmly. There was a scarcely audible click and under her pressure the big door opened.

A flood of warm air greeted her as she stepped across the threshold into the hall and softly shut the door. It was very dark here and very still. The only sound that broke the silence was the muffled ticking of a clock from somewhere close at hand.

The Angel dropped the key, which she had retained, back into her pocket and drew out an electric torch no bigger than a large fountain pen. Its thin ribbon of light flickered through the darkness moving back and forth as she sought for the position of the stairway. It faced the hall door, a thickly carpeted staircase of black oak that blended with the panelling of the walls and was lost in the shadows above.

Montgomery Webb's study, and her objective, was on the first floor, a room with a balcony that overlooked the porch. Mr. Webb was fond of boasting about his possessions and it had been ridiculously easy to acquire all the information she wanted.

The door of the room she was seeking was the last on the right and her hand was on the handle when she heard a muffled sound and went rigid. The soft-toned note of a gong reassured her. The noise that had startled her had only

27

been the mechanism of the clock below as it prepared to strike.

She released her suddenly pent breath, and then there came to her ears another sound, this time from within the room she was about to enter. There was no mistaking what it was; that faint rustling could only have been made by somebody sorting papers.

Angela stood motionless, every nerve in her body tense. Who was in the room beyond the closed door? Had Montgomery Webb broken his usual rule and sat up late?

Swiftly and noiselessly she stooped until her eyes were on a level with the keyhole, but she could see nothing. Either the room was in darkness or more likely, the key on the inside obstructed the tiny aperture. She knelt on the soft pile of the carpet, but no light came from under the door either, and there was quite an appreciable space. If there had been any normal light in that room it could not have failed to be visible.

Her level brows drew together in a little frown and she pursed her lips. It was queer. If it was Montgomery Webb in that room, he would surely have put on the light. He would scarcely be examining papers in the dark. And if it wasn't Webb, who was it?

She rose carefully to her feet. Was it an inquisitive or dishonest servant? Or somebody on a similar errand to herself?

She could hear nothing now from the room. Once more there was complete and utter silence. For a moment she considered what she should do. She was reluctant, having come so far, to turn back without having accomplished her object. She came to a decision.

Swiftly she pulled the brim of her hat farther down over her eyes. The fingers of her right hand dipped into her pocket and closed round the hard butt of her tiny automatic as she gently pushed the door open an inch.

In spite of the risk, she felt she must have light. With her left hand she groped frantically for the switch and found it, as she had expected, just inside the doorway. A second later and the room was flooded with light. It was empty. And then, as she saw the chaotic confusion that surrounded her, she drew in her breath quickly.

The large apartment was strewn with papers, papers that had come from the open drawers of the big pedestal desk that stood near the french windows opening on to the balcony. A wall safe was open, and in front of it was a confused litter of account books, documents, and money, banknotes, which had apparently come from a black cashbox, the lid of which had been wrenched ruthlessly open. By a remarkable coincidence she had apparently chosen the same night as another burglar who had marked Mr. Montgomery Webb's house for his operations. It must have been he whom she had heard. And now she saw that one of the long windows was ajar. That was the way the intruder had made his escape.

The little leather roll against her hip containing the diamond-sharp drill and delicate steel instruments with which she had armed herself would not now be needed. In that confusion on the floor she might find what she was seeking.

She moved forward cautiously with the intention of conducting a swift search. But the intention was never carried out. As she rounded the desk she saw a foot — a slippered foot with six inches of bare ankle protruding from the leg of a gaudy suit of pyjamas. On the floor, hidden from her previous view by the big desk, lay Montgomery Webb. His heavy face was upturned and there was blood on the bald head. She only had to look once to know that he was dead. No man with such a wound could have remained alive. The top of his skull had been crushed like an eggshell.

She stared down at the obese, obscene figure, the blood drained from her face and her eyes wide with horror. And then suddenly, like a douche of cold water, she realised her position. If she were found, nothing could save her being accused of the murder. She had been in Montgomery Webb's company that evening; she remembered the sight of the man in the opposite box, which had given her a momentary qualm of uneasiness. He would remember. It was his business to remember. Safety lay in getting out of that room and out of that house as quickly as she could.

She forced herself to be calm, and going over to the door switched out the light. The sound of a car coming up the drive reached her ears.

She stood, listening. It came nearer, stopped!

There was a moment's pause and then a loud, imperative knocking rang through the house.

With swift, noiseless steps the Angel crossed to the window. Peering down, she saw the headlights of the car and the vague figures of several men. She caught the glimpse of a uniform and caught her breath. And then a tall man stepped back from the shadow of the porch and looked up. There was now no doubt. The car contained detectives. She had recognised the man who had looked up. It was the man who had sat in the opposite box — Detective-Inspector Holland!

4

A Call From the Yard

Coming out of the Mayfair Theatre, Jimmy Holland saw the departure of the Angel and her elderly escort, and remarked upon the fact to Freddie Babbington.

'What a girl like that can see in a bald-headed old baboon with one foot in the grave beats me!' declared that disgusted individual, staring after the expensive car. 'It isn't natural!'

Jimmy grinned as he looked round in search of an empty taxi.

He caught sight of a cab, whistled, and elbowed his way through the crowd in its direction.

'St. Mark's Mansions, Ryder Street,' he said to the driver, as he pulled open the door.

'Here, what's the idea?' protested Freddie, in consternation. 'You're not going home yet, surely?'

'I am, my lad,' retorted Jimmy decisively. 'I've got a hard day's work before me tomorrow.'

'It is useless,' said Freddie Babbington, apostrophising the world at large, 'for a simple and innocent citizen like myself to argue with a man whose finer instincts have become coarsened by constant association with the cunning and unscrupulous machinations of the law. I capitulate!'

He followed Jimmy into the taxi, and the grinning driver let in his clutch. Limpet admitted them when they arrived, and the faintest expression of surprise appeared on his benevolent face.

'I did not anticipate your return at such an early hour, sir,' he remarked deferentially, as he took their coats and hats.

'Of course you didn't, Limpet!' cried Freddie. 'And, believe me, it wasn't my fault. I did my best to persuade Mr. Holland to round off the evening in a manner appropriate to the occasion.'

'I'm sure you did, sir,' said Limpet respectfully.

'But I nobly resisted the temptation,' put in Jimmy. 'Your aspirin will not be required. Bring the whiskey and some sandwiches into my study.'

'Very good, sir.' Limpet bowed and moved majestically away as Jimmy took his friend by the arm and led him into the cosy room in which he spent most of his time when he was at home.

'This,' he said, with a sigh of content, when the whiskey had been brought and they were seated comfortably in front of the glowing warmth of the electric radiator — 'this is much better, in my opinion, than a noisy place like the Café de France.'

Freddie Babbington took a prodigious gulp at his drink, and set down his half-empty glass on the small table between them.

'I'm not sure you aren't right,' he agreed, leaning back in his chair lazily. 'Tell me, James, did you mean what you said about that girl in the theatre?'

'I should hardly say a thing like that unless I did mean it,' answered Jimmy gravely.

'It sounds incredible to me!' The other's round, good-humoured face was unusually serious. 'Completely incredible! That a girl with a face like that should be a crook is — unbelievable!'

'Surely you've lived long enough to know that looks mean nothing?' said Jimmy. 'Especially where women are concerned.'

'Yes, but — ' Babbington shook his head. 'That girl! What did you say her name was — Angela Kesson? She was lovely, Jimmy. There was nothing hard or calculating about her face. It was almost — almost spiritual!'

'That's probably her stock-in-trade,' said Jimmy cynically.

'I'd have sworn it wasn't put on!' declared Freddie. He stretched out an arm and his fingers played with his glass. 'What do you know about her?' he continued abruptly. 'Not suspect — actually know?'

Jimmy Holland helped himself to a cigar and began to remove the band.

'Well, I actually know very little,' he confessed, after a pause. 'I don't think anybody knows very much about her.'

'You must know something, or you wouldn't have said she was the cleverest thief in London,' persisted Freddie.

'I didn't,' said Jimmy, carefully piercing the end of his cigar with a match. 'I said I had every reason to believe so.'

The other made an impatient gesture.

'That's only quibbling!' he said. 'It amounts to the same thing.'

'You're very interested, aren't you?' remarked his friend, raising his eyebrows quizzically.

'Yes, I am. Jolly interested,' said Babbington. 'I've never seen any girl who — who made such an impression on me!' His tone was half defiant and half embarrassed.

'Take my advice, then,' said Jimmy quietly, 'and forget it, Freddie.' He stuck the cigar between his teeth and lit it. 'The less interested you are in the Angel the better for you.'

'Tell me what you know about her,' said Babbington again, and Jimmy hesitated.

This big, red-faced man who sprawled

opposite him was rather childish in some ways. Unless he was disillusioned at the outset, this sudden infatuation for Angela Kesson might easily lead to a great deal of trouble. And Jimmy was sufficiently fond of him to try to avert any such unpleasant contingency.

'You'll have to promise to treat anything I tell you as strictly confidential,' he said, after a pause.

'Of course — naturally.' Freddie nodded. 'Don't worry about that. Go ahead.'

'Well, then,' continued his friend, 'the reason I advise you to forget all about Angela Kesson is because people who have been friendly with that charming little lady have all been curiously unlucky.'

'How d'you mean?' demanded Freddie quickly.

'I'll tell you if you'll only keep quiet,' said Jimmy. 'We first became interested in Angela Kesson just over eight months ago. We're naturally interested in anyone who is the least bit mysterious, and mystery and the Angel are as inseparable as Swann & Edgar.' He blew out a cloud of smoke and went on: 'Much as you may think to the contrary, Scotland Yard doesn't like mysteries, and you must admit that there is something mysterious about a girl who chooses her male acquaintances from among men with, to put it mildly, undesirable reputations, and when, in every instance, shortly after they have become friendly with her, their houses have been burgled.'

'Burgled!' exclaimed Babbington, and Jimmy nodded.

'Yes,' he answered. 'And this isn't suspicion, it's fact! Abel Scarthright's house at Kingston was broken into and two thousand pounds in notes stolen, seven months ago, and he had made the acquaintance of Angela Kesson a week previously. Julian Hathaway lost a lot of jewellery and fifteen hundred pounds from his flat in Montague Street a month later, and he was seen in the company of the Angel a fortnight before the robbery took place. The same thing happened with Oscar Leeming, and also with Daniel Phelps and old Jonathan Bellman. They all became friendly with the Angel, and they were all robbed of varying amounts.'

'But you've no proof she was responsible!' said Babbington. 'Dash it all, there's such a thing as coincidence!'

'If you believe the same thing could happen five times you're a goop!' said Jimmy candidly.

'But I mean to say!' protested Freddie obstinately. 'You've absolutely no proof that this girl had anything to do with the robberies!'

'I admitted that at the beginning,' said his friend. 'But by all the laws of probability, it's queer. And there's another thing that's also queer. She lives in an expensive flat in Wyvern Court, near Baker Street. She buys the best of everything. She has her clothes made in Paris. Where does the money come from?'

'She may have a private income?' suggested Freddie.

'She hasn't,' answered Jimmy shortly. 'We have ways and means of finding out these things, and when she first came under our notice we made inquiries. No, I'm afraid, old man, you've got to believe me when I tell you that Angela Kesson is best left severely alone.'

'Most of what you have said against her could be explained away,' said Babbington.

'You're an obstinate old ass, aren't you?' grunted Jimmy. 'Explain why she mixes with these men, who are all on our suspected list. Explain why she consorts with known criminals, who have all been 'inside' for some offence or other. Explain why even her maid has a brother who is at present serving a sentence for burglary. Explain all that and reconcile it with innocence and I'll reconsider my remarks.'

Freddie's reply was characteristic.

'Why do you call her the Angel?' he asked.

'My sergeant gave her that name for reasons which are obvious,' answered Jimmy, 'and the name's got around.'

Babbington helped himself to more whiskey.

'And you seriously think,' he remarked, as he splashed soda into the glass, 'that this girl is responsible for all these burglaries?'

'Yes, indirectly,' affirmed his friend. 'I don't suggest she does them herself, but

I believe she's in with a gang who use her as a decoy.'

Freddie opened his mouth to continue the argument, but before he had time to speak the telephone bell rang.

'Excuse me,' muttered Jimmy, and went over to the instrument. For ten minutes he held a rather staccato conversation with the late caller, and then he hung up the receiver and turned.

'That's a coincidence, if you like,' he said. 'You know that man whom the Angel was with tonight?'

Freddie nodded.

'You remember me telling you he was suspected of being a crook?' went on Jimmy. 'Well, the suspicion was apparently well founded. He's a blackmailer, and somebody's squealed. We're raiding his house tonight. We've been told we shall find all the proof we want there. I'll have to turn you out now, old man. I've got to go along to the Yard.'

5

The Photograph

Instinctively the Angel drew back from the window, although the man below could not possibly have seen her.

Detective-Inspector Holland, of Scotland Yard, and the cleverest man in the C.I.D.? What had brought him to this house in the small hours of the morning? He couldn't be already aware of what lay in the study. There must be some other reason. But there was no time to waste conjecturing. She must get away before his knocking roused the servants.

She stepped away from the window and turned back into the room in which Montgomery Webb lay dead. The front way was useless as a means of escape — she would be seen immediately — but another window with a balcony at one side offered a possibility.

She tiptoed across the darkened room,

picking her way over the debris of papers that littered the floor, carefully. The long windows were unfastened, and with a gloved hand she pushed the right leaf open, stepping on to the stone balcony.

As she did so, she trod on something that lay just outside the window. Looking quickly down to see what it was, she made out a dim, square object, and stooping, picked it up. With difficulty she saw it was a mounted photograph. It seemed, from its appearance, to be of the Victorian era and there was some sprawling writing across one corner. Had the killer dropped it?

The sound of whispering from below attracted her attention, and, mechanically thrusting the photograph into her blouse, she peered over the balustrade. There were men moving in the garden underneath! Escape that way was cut off.

The house was obviously surrounded, and any attempt to leave it by either back or front was impossible without being seen. But leave it she must — and quickly.

The booming sound of renewed knocking reached her. At any moment the servants would wake up, and the police would be admitted. They would discover that sprawling thing, stiffening in the study and all the explaining in the world wouldn't make them believe that she had not been responsible. In spite of her steady nerve, she gave a little shiver.

She slipped back into the room, took out her tiny torch and being careful to shield the light from the window, sent the ray dancing about the room. Her memory had not been at fault. There was a door opposite the fireplace. She went over quickly and turned the handle. The door opened and she found, as she had hoped and expected, that she was in Montgomery Webb's bedroom. She closed the communicating door behind her and turned the key. Crossing to another door, which obviously opened into the corridor, she made sure that that was locked also, and began to put the plan that had occurred to her into execution.

By the light of her torch she found the wardrobe and hastily removed a lounge suit and a mackintosh, which she flung on the bed. On a rack were several hats and she selected a grey trilby and threw it beside the other things. Swiftly, working in the dark, she took off her jacket and skirt, pulled on a pair of trousers and struggled into a coat and waistcoat. Fortunately Montgomery Webb had been stout, and there was ample room in the top of the trousers to thrust her costume. Tucking up her hair under the soft felt hat, she put on the mackintosh, switched on her torch and took a quick peep at herself in the long mirror. She saw a passable representation of a fattish man — passable enough, anyway, in the half dark. Her own scarf she tied round mouth and nose, and gripping her small automatic, unlocked the corridor door and slipped out.

From somewhere she heard the sound of excited voices and guessed that at last the servants had been roused from their slumbers. The hall, however was still in darkness, and for this she breathed a sigh of thankfulness as she sped quickly down the broad staircase. Heavy footsteps came to her from somewhere above as she hurriedly concealed herself behind a large coat stand and waited. A light suddenly came on, shedding a soft radiance over the hall, and a large, plump man with dishevelled hair, his ample form enveloped in a dressing gown, appeared on the stairs. He descended slowly, crossed the hall, and opened the front door.

'What is it?' he demanded in a thick voice that was still husky with sleep. 'What the dickens do you mean making all this row in the middle of the night?'

'I'm Detective-Inspector Holland, of Scotland Yard.' The Angel saw the speaker as he stepped into the light. 'Is Mr. Montgomery Webb in?'

'Of course he's in — in bed,' answered the man in the dressing gown. 'Where else do you expect him to be at this hour?'

He was still angry and evidently by no means awed by the identity of the disturber of his sleep.

'Fetch him!' was the curt answer.

'What for — ?' began the plump man truculently.

'I have a warrant to search this house for incriminating evidence,' came the

47

reply. 'Please wake Mr. Webb at once!'

The watching girl saw the plump man's jaw drop, and his rather large eyes bulge in shocked amazement.

'Search — search — this house!' he stammered. 'Strewth!'

He turned abruptly and ambled away.

A hoarse cry came from upstairs, and the Angel stiffened. There was the thudding of feet, and the plump man came flying down the stairs, his face a pasty white, his dressing gown streaming out behind him and revealing a gaudy suit of pyjamas.

'My God! My God!' he croaked hoarsely.

'Here, what's the matter?' The young inspector turned sharply.

'The master — Mr. Webb!' cried the plump man huskily. 'He's dead — in his study! His head's all over blood — !'

'Steady, man!' The detective gripped his arm. What's all this? Mr. Webb dead?'

The servant nodded.

'On the floor by his desk,' he muttered. 'And his head — awful — '

'Take me to him at once!' ordered the

detective. 'You'd better come.'

The man to whom he had been speaking appeared in the open doorway — a small, red-faced man with a smear of reddish-gold moustache.

The Angel held her breath. This was the moment she had been waiting for — hoping for. The three mounted the stairs; leaving the hall empty. She came cautiously from her hiding place, and after a second's hesitation walked boldly out of the open front door.

The police car was drawn up near the steps, but there was no one in sight. The other men she had seen were most probably found at the back. She set off down the drive, and was passing the stationary car when a voice hailed her.

'Here, you! Who are you, and where are you goin'?'

A man's head was thrust out from the driving seat.

'Nobody can't leave this house without permission — inspector's orders!'

The Angel waited to hear no more. She took to her heels and sped down the dark drive as fast as she could run. A shout followed her, and a whistle shrilled. She flew out of the gate and turned towards the place where she had left her car, praying that no suspicious policeman would be waiting near. To her relief, there was nobody. Breathlessly she climbed into the driving seat and started the engine.

The car moved forward, and as she set its long radiator in the direction of London she let her strained nerves relax. She had just passed through one of the worst hours of her life.

Cordelia Smith, heavy-eyed and yawning, was waiting up for her.

'So you 'ave got back! That's a bit o' luck!' she remarked, as Angela closed the door of the flat; and then her small eyes opened very wide. 'Blimey!' she expostulated. 'What 'ave yer been doin' to yerself? Where'd you get them togs?'

She went into her bedroom and divested herself of her uncomfortable attire. It had served its purpose, and Cordelia could burn the whole outfit in the furnace of the central heating plant that supplied warmth to the block of flats, first thing in the morning. Taking off her blouse, she found the photograph she had picked up on the balcony. It was old-fashioned, as she had thought. An elderly man with side-whiskers was lounging gracefully on the back of a gilt chair. Behind him hung a heavy velvet curtain, draped artistically to reveal a large aspidistra on a marble pedestal. Across the corner in ink that had gone brown with age was an inscription:

'With love from Uncle Ebenezer.'

Angela made a grimace at the photograph and dropped it into a drawer of her dressing table, unaware that its possession was to bring into her life a danger that surpassed any she had known and very nearly cause her to share the same fate as that which had overtaken Mr. Montgomery Webb.

6

The Handkerchief

Jimmy Holland stood staring down at the ugly figure with its battered head, and his face was stern.

Whatever Montgomery Webb had been — and Jimmy had heard things that night which suggested he had been pretty bad — this was a dreadful end to come to. That it was murder there was no doubt at all. The state of the room and the gravity of the wound testified to that. It was also fairly easy to guess what had happened. Somebody had broken in, and Webb, sleeping in the adjoining bedroom, had been disturbed, had come to investigate, and had been killed before he could raise an alarm.

'You'd better get on to the Divisional Police,' said Jimmy to the red-haired sergeant, who was standing at his elbow. 'Ask them to bring the police doctor with them. There's a telephone on the desk.'

Sergeant Scorby nodded, and went over to the instrument.

'Police station — and look sharp!' he barked into the mouthpiece. He invariably barked, under the illusion that staccatoism was a sign of efficiency. Just as he had got his connection, a whistle shrilled sharply from outside, and Jimmy turned quickly.

'Stay where you are!' he snapped to the shivering man in the dressing gown, who was hovering in the open doorway, his fat face a dirty grey and his bulging eyes fearful. 'Don't go into the room until I come back.'

He pushed past the bulky form, almost cannoned into three partly dressed women, who were huddled together in the corridor, and dashed down the stairs. One of his men met him as he came out of the door.

'Who blew that whistle?' asked Jimmy sharply.

'Simmonds, sir,' answered the detective. 'I was round at the back with Johnson. What happened — ?'

'Murder!' snapped his superior, and went over to the police car. A glance showed him that it was empty. He stared about, but could see no sign of Detective-Constable Simmonds.

'What the devil did he blow his whistle for?' he muttered.

The man with him took the remark for a question addressed to himself

'I don't know, sir — ' he began, and stopped, for Jimmy was no longer at his side. He had seen a movement near the entrance to the drive and had gone to investigate. He discovered a breathless Simmonds returning.

'I lost him!' gasped the man disappointedly.

'Lost him? Lost who?' demanded Jimmy ungrammatically.

With difficulty, for his sprint had partially winded him, Simmonds explained.

'He was a fattish fellow, with his face covered by a coloured scarf,' he concluded. 'And lor' — how he could run!'

'He was also a murderer!' said Jimmy, and the man gaped at him. 'Montgomery Webb's dead, and his study is like a junk-shop. Ten to one that fellow you saw is responsible.'

He turned away and went back to the death room.

'The Divisional Inspector is coming right away, sir,' greeted Sergeant Scorby smartly. 'Ambulance and doctor with him. What was the racket?'

Jimmy told him.

'Murderer was here when we arrived, eh?' grunted the sergeant. 'Pity Simmonds missed him, sir.'

'A great pity,' agreed Jimmy. 'While we are waiting for the local men, we might have a look through this mess.'

They set to work on the chaos, and they had not got very far before Jimmy came to the conclusion that the person who had killed Mr. Webb had done that unpleasant gentleman a good turn. There was enough evidence among that litter to have sent him down for fifteen years. It was obvious that blackmail had been his speciality, though he had apparently dabbled in a little fencing as a profitable sideline. His business in the City appeared to have been used merely as a cloak to cover his real activities — a fact which the police had long suspected. And here was proof, irrefutable proof. Without doubt his death had saved Mr. Montgomery a great deal of trouble and discomfort.

'Look after all those documents carefully,' said Jimmy, as he made a neat parcel of certain papers relating to the unfortunate people whom the dead man had been squeezing. 'We shall have to interview all these people. It's my opinion that one of them killed him.'

The divisional-inspector and the doctor arrived at that moment, and Jimmy explained the circumstances of the crime.

'I've always thought there was something fishy about Webb,' remarked Inspector Sharpe, rubbing his long, thin nose. 'Blackmailer, was he? Humph! Well, I'm not surprised.'

While the doctor was making his examination, Jimmy, the local man, and Scorby conducted a search of the room. It was the sergeant who discovered the open window and the scratches on the hasp.

'That's the way he got in, sir,' he

declared — and Jimmy and Sharpe went over to the little balcony.

'Easy,' remarked the local inspector. 'He only had to climb on to that window ledge, pull himself up by the balustrade, and he was practically in the room.'

There was no clue to the identity of the killer, however, and they came back to find that the doctor had completed his preliminary inspection.

'He was killed by a heavy blow from behind,' said the divisional-surgeon, and launched into a highly technical description of the dead man's injuries. 'He must have died almost at once. I don't suppose he even knew who killed him.'

'Then he's in much the same position as we are, doctor,' said Jimmy ruefully. 'I suppose this door leads into his bedroom.'

He went over, turned the handle, and discovered to his surprise that the door was locked.

'That's funny,' he muttered, frowning.

'Why is it funny, sir?' asked Sergeant Scorby, at his elbow.

'Well, it seems pretty obvious that he was disturbed, and came to discover the cause,' explained his superior. 'You'd think he'd take the shortest route, which was through the door, but it's locked on the inside.'

'Maybe he always kept it locked?' suggested Sharpe.

Jimmy shook his head doubtfully, and went out into the corridor. The servants were whispering together in a frightened group, watched by a stolid constable.

'Was that your master's bedroom?' Jimmy addressed the plump-faced man and pointed to the door adjoining the study.

'Yes, sir,' replied the man tremulously.

Jimmy went to the door, saw that it was ajar, and pushed it open. The room beyond was in darkness, but he found the switch and pressed it down. As the room became illuminated he gave a quick glance round. The bed was rumpled, the coverlet flung back, and the door of a large wardrobe stood open. Jimmy's eyes narrowed and he went swiftly over to the massive cupboard. There were hangers with many suits inside, but they all looked curiously disturbed and untidy. Had Mr. Webb been responsible before he went to bed, or — He called to the plump-faced man, and he came reluctantly.

'Do you know anything about your master's clothes?' asked Jimmy sharply.

The servant nodded.

'Yes, sir. I used to valet him,' he answered,

'Then take a look at this wardrobe and tell me if there is anything missing?' snapped Jimmy.

The other's eyes widened.

'Missing — ' he began.

'Yes!' broke in Jimmy curtly, and turned to make a search of the room. He found two little scraps of mud near the bed, and amongst the rumpled sheets made a more important discovery. It was a small square of lace-edged linen — a woman's handkerchief, and an expensive one.

His mind flew to the girl with whom the dead man had spent the evening. Was she in this business? It looked very much as if at some time or other she had been in this room. He examined the handkerchief, but there were no initials. There was, however, a faint perfume, and it was an expensive scent, which Jimmy recognised. It had just become fashionable, and was called 'Sans Adieu'.

'Did your master come home alone tonight?' he inquired, and the servant, who was busy at the wardrobe, turned.

'Yes, sir,' he answered.

So the Angel, if the handkerchief had belonged to her, had not accompanied Webb home after the theatre. But that didn't say she had not come later. He put the handkerchief away in his pocket.

'There's a suit, a mackintosh, and a hat missing from here, sir,' said the plump-faced man suddenly.

Jimmy was instantly alert.

'Describe them,' he said, and the man did so.

The description coincided with the apparel worn by the man whom Simmonds had chased down the drive.

Jimmy pursed his lips. There was no need for a man to have changed his clothes. But if it had been a woman who wished to be mistaken for a man —

'Miss Kesson,' he muttered to himself, 'I'm going to give myself the pleasure of interviewing you in the morning, and I think the pleasure will be all on my side!'

7

Jimmy Meets the Angel

A vigorous shaking startled Angela Kesson out of a deep sleep, and she sat up yawning, to find Cordelia at the bedside with a cup of tea.

'What time is it?' demanded the Angel, her voice heavy with sleep.

'It's gone nine,' answered the maid, 'and it's rainin' like 'ell! Drink yer tea and I'll put yer bath on.'

Angela took the cup and scalded herself to wakefulness.

She was having breakfast before the fire in the cosy sitting room when the knock came at the door, and after a pause Cordelia entered with a troubled face.

'I knew it 'ud come one of these fine days,' she whispered, closing the door. 'An' now it 'as!'

'What has?' demanded the Angel.

'Ther perlice!' replied the maid. 'There's

61

a 'busy' in the 'all now, an' 'e wants ter see yer.'

She thrust a card under her mistress' nose and Angela glanced at the super-scription.

'Show Inspector Holland in,' said Angela quietly, and reluctantly the maid obeyed.

Jimmy Holland entered the prettily furnished room and was greeted with a dazzling smile.

'Good morning, inspector!' said the Angel sweetly. 'Do sit down, won't you?'

'Thank you.' Jimmy bowed a little distantly and took the chair her hand indicated. His manner was polite but frigid, and Angela's eyes gleamed wick-edly.

'Would you like some coffee, or anything?' she asked.

'No, thank you!' He shook his head.

'You don't mind if I go on with my breakfast?' she inquired. 'I'm afraid I'm a little later than usual!'

'Please do,' he said. 'No doubt you went to bed rather later — than usual?'

'How clever of you to guess that. But,

of course, you're a detective, aren't you?' There was exaggerated awe in her voice, and Jimmy felt himself redden, and was annoyed.

'Yes, I'm a detective,' he said. 'That is the reason I'm here. The fact is, Miss Kesson, I should like you to answer a few questions.'

'Questions?' repeated the Angel, her grey eyes widening innocently. 'What questions? I haven't been doing anything against the law, have I, inspector?'

'You should be better able to know that!' retorted Jimmy. 'You were at the Mayfair last night with Montgomery Webb?'

'I was. You saw me. You were in the opposite box,' said Angela. 'It was quite a good show, wasn't it?'

'It was,' agreed Jimmy. 'But I didn't come here to discuss its merits.'

'I'm still waiting to hear what you did come for,' she said, delicately nibbling at a piece of toast.

'I came to ask you for an account of your movements after you left the theatre,' he answered.

She raised her eyebrows.

'Really, Inspector — er — Holland,' she said, a little coldly, 'that appears to be my business.'

'I'm afraid it's also mine!' retorted Jimmy. 'I can't force you to answer, of course, if you refuse. But I'm investigating a serious crime, and your evidence may be helpful.'

He was watching her narrowly, but her lovely face remained impassive, except for a faint expression of quite a natural surprise.

'A serious crime?' she repeated.

'It would be difficult to find a more serious one,' he replied curtly. 'Murder!'

She caught her breath and stared at him.

'But how dreadful!' She lowered her voice. 'Still, I don't understand how I —

'Mr. Montgomery Webb was murdered in the early hours of this morning with his head battered in!'

She put up a hand to her slender throat.

'Mr. Webb?' she whispered. 'It seems — it seems impossible — '

'It's true, all the same,' said Jimmy. 'And I want to know when you left him and what you did after.'

'Poor man and he was so cheerful — ' she began; and then suddenly she seemed to realize the point of his question. 'Oh, but you're not — you can't be thinking that I had anything to — to — '

'I'm not thinking anything, Miss Kesson,' said Jimmy, as she hesitated. 'I'm only making inquiries.'

'I'm afraid I can't help you very much,' she said doubtfully. 'Mr. Webb drove me home after the theatre, and I went to bed.'

'Straight to bed?' inquired Jimmy.

'Well, no,' she answered. 'I wasn't very tired, and I wrote some letters and read for a little while.'

'You didn't go out again?' he insisted.

'Why, of course not!' she replied. 'It was after twelve before I got home.'

'And you didn't see Webb again after you said goodnight at the door?'

'Of course I didn't. I left him in his car. He said he was going home.'

'Supposing I told you,' he said, eyeing

her steadily, 'that I have evidence to prove that you did go out again and that you went to Webb's house, what would you say?'

'I should say that you were mistaken,' answered Angela, coolly returning his gaze. 'Which would be more polite than suggesting that you were mad?'

She reached towards a box on a table at her side and helped herself to a cigarette. Her fingers were quite steady as she lit it and blew a thin stream from her red lips.

'Are you satisfied?' she asked.

'No, I'm not!' he snapped. 'I believe you were at Webb's house last night. I believe that you were there when I arrived, and that you escaped by dressing yourself in a suit of his clothes — '

He stopped as she began to laugh softly.

'Really, Mr. Holland,' she said, 'you're the most amusing man I've ever met. What a ridiculous suggestion to make!'

'Is it ridiculous?' he asked. 'Can you prove that what I've said isn't true?'

'Can you prove that it is?' she retorted. 'You've been reading too many detective stories. I had nothing to do with the murder. Why should I want to kill the poor man, anyhow? He was rather a bore, but that's not a reasonable motive for killing him. I'm afraid, Mr. Holland, you're wasting quite a lot of time over me!'

'If you weren't at Webb's house, how did your handkerchief come to be found in his bedroom?' he demanded.

She raised her eyebrows.

'Was it?' she said. 'It sounds a little indelicate, anyway.'

He put his hand into his breast pocket and took out the little square of lace-edged linen.

'Isn't that yours?' he asked.

She looked at it curiously.

'Yes, it's one of mine,' she admitted. 'But it has no initials. How could you tell?'

'I wasn't certain until I entered this flat,' he answered. 'But the scent of Sans Adieu is unmistakable — '

Again she interrupted him by laughing.

'My dear man,' she said, 'quite half the women in London are using Sans Adieu. It's the latest rage. I've been thinking of giving it up because it's becoming too common. You may be a very good detective, but you don't know much about the habits of women.' She smiled at him, her eyes alight with amusement, and he thought he had never seen anything more attractive.

'But this is yours?' he said, and she nodded.

'Yes. I'm afraid poor Mr. Webb must have been a trifle sentimental. Fancy taking my handkerchief as a souvenir. Or perhaps I'm misjudging him and I dropped it in the car.'

8

The Man Who Came by Night

Jimmy Holland looked at the lovely mocking face of the girl before him and felt a little foolish. Here was an explanation for the presence of that handkerchief which had not occurred to him — an explanation, moreover, that was reasonable and likely. If it had been anyone else but the Angel he would have apologised and taken his leave there and then. But the rumours that had circulated about her must have some element of truth. The unimaginative men at the Yard were not in the habit of suspecting people without a just and tangible cause, and there was no doubt that her record was peculiar, to say the least of it.

'So that is your explanation,' he said quietly.

'It's the only sensible one,' she answered. 'Since I certainly did not take the handkerchief to Mr. Webb's house, he must have taken it there himself.'

She was laughing at him. He saw the amusement in her eyes and was unusually embarrassed.

'You have a car, haven't you?' he asked, and when she nodded, 'What garage do you keep it at?'

'You take a lot of convincing,' she said. 'It must be very unpleasant to have such a suspicious nature. Harker's, in South Street. The telephone is beside you. Why not ring them up and ask if I took my car out last night, which is what you're dying to know. It'll ease your mind.'

She was quite safe in suggesting this, for the man who ran Harker's was merely a nominee for herself, and he had received his instructions that morning.

Jimmy made a wry grimace, and then grinned.

'I don't think I'll bother, since you're so pressing,' he said, rising to his feet. 'I seem to have been barking up the wrong tree.'

'I think you have, rather,' she agreed. 'All the same, I'm grateful to you. It's been rather amusing.'

He left, carrying with him a memory of laughing grey eyes and a lovely mocking smile that was altogether charming and adorable. He called in to Harker's all the same and put his question, though he expected and received a negative answer.

The Angel left her flat a few minutes later and walked round to the garage for her car, and the man whom Jimmy had left for that specific purpose followed at a respectful distance. Mr. Harker, a red-faced sandy-haired man came forward from a small office to attend to her personally as she walked into the yard.

'Good-mornin', miss,' he said, rubbing his grease-covered hands down the leg of an even greasier pair of overalls. 'Want your car?'

'Yes, please,' she answered.

'Hi, Ginger! Miss Kesson wants 'er car,' yelled Mr. Harker and was answered by a muffled voice from under a big saloon.

'She's been filled up,' said Mr. Harker, and then looking quickly about him added in a hoarse whisper: 'There was a feller 'ere this mornin' askin' if you'd 'ad 'er out last night.'

'Oh, then he did come,' murmured the Angel.

'Yes, miss.' Mr. Harker nodded quickly. ' 'E didn't get no change out 'o me, though,' he grinned, showing a row of broken yellow teeth.

'Presumably he'll come again,' said the girl. 'There's a man outside now who's followed me from the flat.'

Mr. Harker screwed up his eyes and stared at the entrance to the yard.

'I can't see no one, miss,' he said.

'He's there all the same,' said Angela calmly. 'I hope he enjoys himself. He doesn't worry me.'

'Ginger' appeared at that moment, a long, thin, weedy youth with a face that was black with oil.

'Shall I push the car out for you?' he inquired.

'Please,' said Angela. 'Stick to your story, Tom,' she went on, turning again to Mr. Harker. 'The car wasn't out last night.'

'You bet your life I will, miss,' he said,

'and so will my boy. We ain't forgot, miss.'

She laid her hand on his arm.

'I know I can always rely on you, Tom,' she said, and moved away to climb into the car, which Ginger had just brought out.

Mr. Harker watched the long machine and its dainty driver disappear out of the yard, and turned to his son.

'That's a girl in a million, boy,' he said. 'That's a real lady. There ain't many like 'er, son. She's got guts!'

The Angel lunched leisurely at the Chatham Grill and then drove slowly into Berkshire. She came presently to a small village as yet unspoiled by the ubiquitous builder, though there were signs that his encroachment would not be postponed for long, and negotiating the narrow streets, stopped her car near a tiny church that crowned the brow of the hill. It was an aged building, nestling amid an ancient graveyard to which curiously clipped yew-trees gave an old-world atmosphere.

The Angel stood for a moment or two by the lychgate, eyeing the scene wistfully and with an expression that had grown very soft; and then she opened the gate and passed through. It was very quiet and peaceful here in this old burial ground with the grass-grown mounds and crumbling stones. There was no one about, no sound except the twittering of the birds in the big oak-trees that had been old when the first grave had been dug. An air of peace and tranquility. London, with its bustle and rush and noise, seemed very distant — almost to belong to another age.

The girl walked slowly along the little path, skirted the church, and came to the more modern portion of the graveyard. Here, instead of grass were flowers, and the headstones were fresh and white. Here the crumbling dust that lay beneath was remembered, and perhaps mourned for a little time at least. Presently this part, too, would become neglected as memory faded. There would be no more flowers; the neat mounds would grow rank and weedy, and the brave monuments fall into decay. That was the real meaning of death, thought the Angel — to be forgotten.

'But I shall never forget!' she vowed silently. 'I shall never forget!'

She came at last to a grave marked only by a simple cross. It was not a new grave, but it had been carefully tended. A sheaf of blood-red roses lay on the green turf — roses that were beginning to fade. The Angel stooped and picked up the dying blossoms, replacing them with the fresh ones she had brought.

And then she turned away and went back to the place where she had left her car. Her weekly task, which was a labour of love, was done.

Cordelia was setting out the tea things on the low table before the fire in the sitting room when her mistress returned.

When she had finished her tea she went into her bedroom and brought back the Victorian photograph, which the murderer of Montgomery Webb had dropped in his flight. Why had he bothered to take it at all? It had puzzled her at the time, and it puzzled her now.

Was it this innocent-looking photograph which the unknown killer had been seeking? It seemed so, since he had taken it with him. Probably he had thrust it under his coat, and it had dropped without knowing it.

She studied it with wrinkled forehead. Who was 'Uncle Ebenezer', and what secret did that faded print hold? A serious one, and a sinister one, or the person who had killed Webb would not have gone to so much trouble and risk to gain possession of it. And his risk had been for nothing. In his panic he had gone without the thing he had come for.

She could make nothing of the photograph, however, except that Uncle Ebenezer must be either dead, or a very old man, if the portrait were he, and after a while she locked it away in a drawer of her little desk.

It continued to occupy her thoughts on and off for the rest of the evening, and she was still wondering when soon after dinner she went to bed.

Her lack of rest on the previous night had left her very tired, and she fell asleep almost at once.

What woke her she never knew, but suddenly she found herself sitting up in bed with all her senses alert. A long, unmusical snore came faintly to her ears, and she smiled in the darkness.

She was slipping down again comfortably when she heard another sound. It came from the adjoining sitting room — a thud, as though someone had knocked over a chair!

The Angel slid gently out of bed, felt for her dressing gown, and pulled it on over her thin nightdress. She found her slippers, and then noiselessly opened the drawer in her little bedside table and took out her tiny automatic. It was loaded, as she knew, and in spite of its size, capable of doing serious damage at close range. Moving over to the door, she opened it and was stepping out into the hall when there came a muttered oath and a terrific crash from the sitting room. It was followed by the sound of a furious struggle. Something hit the door with a bang, and there was a cry of pain, and then the door was flung open and a man burst through.

He staggered into the hall, recovered his balance, wrenched open the front door, and went racing down the stairs.

Angela, paralysed with astonishment, had snapped on the light and was just going after him, when another man appeared from the sitting room — a small, wizened man, in curious-looking clothes.

'If you move I'll shoot!' said the Angel grimly. 'What are you doing in my flat?'

She heard a gasp behind her, and out of the corner of her eye saw Cordelia, a sketchy figure in a flannel nightdress.

'Gaw!' said the maid huskily. 'It's me Brother Bert!'

9

Danger!

The Angel looked from the startled maid to the rather scared, shifty-eyed individual by the sitting room door, and laughed softly.

'So this is Brother Bert, is it?' she remarked. 'I've heard a lot about you, but I never expected to meet you in the flesh — and in the middle of the night.'

It appeared that he had succeeded in escaping from Pentonville that evening by climbing the wall. Owing to his previous good conduct he had been made an orderly, and getting out of the prison had been fairly easy. He had broken into a lock-up shop, which sold second-hand clothing, and exchanged his convict's garb for the ill-fitting suit he was now wearing. He had hoped to find money as well, but he was disappointed. He had lain low in the garden of an empty house, which had been searched by the police who were looking for him, and he had only escaped this vigilance by climbing a tree and remaining there until the search was over. He knew where to find his sister and had made up his mind to seek her out and obtain the money he required. When he judged that it was safe he had made his way westwards, reaching Wyvern Court at a little after one.

It was too risky to come to the front entrance, but he had found the fire-escape, which communicated with the stone balcony at each storey. He had climbed the wall into the courtyard at the back and ascended the iron stairway as far as the balcony belonging to the flat in which he knew he would find his sister. It had seemed to him a piece of good luck when he had found the windows opening on to this balcony ajar. His first impression was that they had been left open by accident. He had slipped cautiously into the room beyond, his intention being to find his sister's room and waken her without disturbing her employer. He was inside before he realised that there was someone else in the room. A man was bending over a desk in the corner, searching it by the tiny glimmer of a torch over which something had been stuck to make it very dim. The man had heard him, and before he knew what was happening had jumped at him.

'The perisher 'it me,' concluded Mr. Smith, rather breathless from his long recital, 'but 'e missed me jaw and only caught me on the shoulder. Then 'e 'ooked it like 'ell. An' that's the truth, if I never moves from this spot!'

The Angel's smooth forehead wrinkled thoughtfully.

She went over to the sitting-room door, pushed it open, and switched on the light. A small chair lay overturned near the open windows, and the bureau in the corner was littered with bills and other documents, which she kept there, but otherwise the apartment presented its usual appearance. The arrival of 'Brother Bert' must have disturbed the mysterious visitor before he had had time to get very far in his search. And what had he been searching for? Certainly he had been no ordinary burglar. And then it came to her. The man had been looking for the photograph of 'Uncle Ebenezer'!

'This brother of yours is going to be a bit of a problem, Cordelia,' remarked Angela thoughtfully.

'Bert always was a perishin' nuisance!' retorted Cordelia candidly. 'Wot the fool wanted to come 'ere for, nobody knows.'

'It was the natural place for him to come,' answered the Angel, 'and that's the trouble. The police know you're his sister, and this is the first place they'll look for him.'

'An' serve 'im right if they finds 'im,' said the maid viciously. 'Did yer ever 'ear of such a fool trick, breakin' out o' jug when e'd only got a month or two more to go?'

'It was rather stupid,' said Angela. 'But all the same, we can't give him up, and I've an idea he might be useful.'

'Now, don't you go gettin' yourself into no more trouble,' advised Cordelia earnestly. 'You've got — '

She broke off with a startled gasp as a loud and peremptory knocking suddenly echoed through the flat.

'My Gaw'!' she whispered. 'It's the perlice — '

The Angel rose swiftly and silently to her feet.

'Put the light out in the hall,' she ordered below her breath, 'and take these tea things into the kitchen. Tell your brother to get into the linen cupboard and keep quiet, and then go to bed and stop there. Quickly, now, and don't make a sound!'

Cordelia picked up the tray and disappeared silently as Angela's hand slid along the wall and pushed up the light switch, plunging the room in darkness.

The knocking came again, louder and more insistent.

The Angel dropped her hand into the pocket of her dressing gown, drew out the little automatic which she had put there after Cordelia had identified 'Brother Bert', and feeling her way to the settee, stuffed it among the cushions. It would be better to get rid of that. The material of her wrap was silk and the bulge of it would show.

Quietly she stepped out into the darkened hall and waited. For the third time the knocker was plied, and after a slight delay she walked towards the front door noisily, switching on the light, and drew back the catch.

'Who is it?' she began in the husky voice of one awakened from a sound sleep. 'What — '

Her arm was gripped and something hard was pressed into her side.

'Keep quiet,' whispered a muffled voice menacingly. 'If you make a sound I'll kill you.'

She saw the figure that loomed out of the gloom of the landing, and for a second her heart stood still. He stepped into the hall, pushing her before him, and softly closed the door.

'Now,' he whispered, his voice muffled behind the mask. 'Give me the photograph.'

She had recovered from the shock of his unexpected appearance, and her brain was cool and clear.

'Who are you?' she began. 'I — '

'Never mind who I am,' he interrupted.

'Give me the photograph.'

'I don't know what you're talking about,' she said, staring at him with just the right expression of mingled surprise and fear. 'What photograph?'

'You know very well,' he answered roughly. 'The photograph I dropped on the balcony of Webb's house and which you picked up.'

'Oh!' She smiled faintly and shook her head; 'I'm afraid you're wasting your time, I haven't got it.'

'Don't lie,' he snarled.

'I'm not lying,' she answered calmly. 'I haven't got it.'

'Then what have you done with it?' he demanded quickly. 'You had it — I saw you pick it up — '

'Because I had it then is no reason why I should have it now,' she retorted. 'Really, you seem to be taking an immense amount of trouble to recover your uncle's photograph — I presume it is your uncle?'

'That's my business!' snapped the other. 'I want that photograph, and I mean to have it — even if I have to treat you the same way as I treated Webb.'

The Angel faced him steadily.

'Then I'm afraid,' she said evenly, 'you will have to go and talk to my bank manager.'

He started, and the eyes above the handkerchief that covered his face hardened.

'What do you mean?' he muttered.

'Surely it was plain enough,' she replied. 'That photograph seemed to me such a valuable antique that I decided it ought to be kept in a place of safety — somewhere where burglars and such unpleasant people would find difficulty in stealing it — so I deposited it at my bank.'

His hand shot out and gripped her arm.

'What do you know?' he asked harshly. 'How did you discover that that photograph was valuable?'

His fingers hurt her but she did not flinch.

'To anyone with an artistic eye,' she answered, 'its value is obvious. The grouping, the graceful pose of Uncle Ebenezer, the life-like rendering of the aspidistra and the detail of the whiskers. A collector would pay fabulous sums for such a masterpiece — '

He ground out an oath between his teeth and the pistol in his hand moved menacingly.

'Stop trying to be funny,' he said. 'I'm not playing a game. I'm serious. Perhaps you don't realise that? I could kill you now and nobody would hear the shot. There's a silencer fixed to this pistol — '

'That wouldn't help you to recover Uncle Ebenezer,' interrupted the Angel. 'Perhaps you don't realise that you are in a more dangerous position than I am?' The remark and her calm attitude disconcerted him.

'This is your second visit here tonight, isn't it?' she went on before he could speak. 'Your first was even less conventional. You came by way of the fire escape and the windows of my sitting room. Unfortunately for you, you were interrupted by another burglar, and still more unfortunately — again for you — I was awakened by the noise and just before you paid your rather melodramatic return visit I telephoned for the police. I'm expecting them to arrive at any moment.'

He muttered a smothered exclamation.

'So you see,' she concluded coolly, 'you're in rather a dangerous position, aren't you?'

'Is this true?' His voice was uneasy, and she knew that he was scared. She shrugged her shoulders.

'If you don't believe me, wait and see,' she invited. 'They'll probably be very pleased to find you here. They're rather keen on catching the murderer of Montgomery Webb.' She heard him draw in his breath sharply.

'You win for the present,' he said thickly. 'But we shall meet again — and soon.'

'Please make it a more convenient time,' murmured the Angel. 'Which way will you go? By the front door or the fire escape?'

'I'll go by the fire escape,' he snarled furiously. 'I suppose you think you're clever?'

'I was always considered so at school,' she answered sweetly, and opened the

88

sitting room door. 'You know the way, don't you?'

He made no reply, but, switching on the light, he backed across the room, keeping her covered until he reached the long windows. Undoing the clasp with his free hand, he paused on the threshold.

'You've beaten me this time,' he said. 'Whether you've been lying or not I don't know and I can't risk waiting to find out. But if you want to avoid further trouble — and bad trouble — you'd better get hold of that photograph. I shall telephone tomorrow and arrange a place and time where you can bring it to me. You understand?'

'I hear what you say,' she answered.

'If you don't' — his voice was husky with rage — 'if you don't, you'll be sorry! I've warned you!'

He turned abruptly and was gone.

10

'The Black Ring'

The murder of Mr. Montgomery Webb came at a time when the newspapers were particularly lacking in sensation. The Press, therefore, hailed its advent with delight, and devoted more prominence and space to it than might otherwise have been the case. Many people who read of the crime shook in their shoes, although their fear was tempered with relief when they learned that the man who had held them in his clutches and squeezed them dry was dead.

To them came a quiet man from Scotland Yard, who courteously but firmly questioned them concerning their various movements on the night when the murder had been committed.

The reports came in to Jimmy Holland, and he read them with disappointment, for there was nothing tangible to advance the inquiry very far.

'I'm inclined to think, sir,' he said at an interview with the Assistant Commissioner, 'that we're going to have difficulty in finding the person who killed Webb; so many people had a motive. It's my opinion that Webb was only a cog in the wheel.'

'How do you mean?' asked Colonel Blair, raising his eyebrows. 'You're not suggesting that there's a gang at work, are you?'

'Something of the sort, sir,' answered the other. 'I believe there's a kind of 'Black Ring' operating, composed of people like Webb, and working on a big scale.'

★ ★ ★

In a private room which he had engaged at the Holborn Restaurant, Mr. Oscar Leeming presided over a luncheon to which he had invited several of his business associates for the sole purpose of deciding what was to be done about the slim girl who called herself Angela Kesson.

'We've all suffered badly,' said Mr.

Leeming, when coffee had been removed and the waiters had taken their departure, 'taken in like children because of a pretty face, an' we've got to do something. That girl's dangerous!'

'What do you think her game is?' asked Julian Hathaway, his thin, bony fingers stripping the band from a cigar.

'That's what worries me,' said Mr. Leeming. 'It wasn't just plain money she was after — I wouldn't worry if that was all — but all my private papers have been carefully examined.'

'So were mine,' put in Abel Scarthright, in his thin voice. 'Luckily, there was nothing that the whole world wouldn't have seen. It never crossed my mind that the girl had anything to do with the burglary, not until we began comparing notes.'

'Exactly.' Mr. Leeming leaned forward, resting his elbow on the table and punctuating his remarks with the stub of his cigar. 'I said just now I didn't know who she was or what she was after. That's true, I don't, but I've got a shrewd suspicion she's connected with somebody who has — er — what shall I say — suffered through one of our little — er — business deals.'

His listeners became intent.

'Well,' said Mr. Leeming, 'I think — and I'm sure you'll agree with me — that this girl is a potential danger and, therefore, should be — removed!'

'You're not suggesting — ' began Hathaway uneasily.

'I'm suggesting nothing — er — messy,' interrupted his host. 'I'm suggesting she should be rendered harmless in a strictly legal and proper manner — by the police.'

The four men at the table stared at him.

'How?' muttered Scarthright.

'By — to use an American expression — a 'frame-up',' said Mr. Leeming smoothly. 'The police are already suspicious of her — if they could secure irrefutable evidence — ' He paused and surveyed his companions with an expansive smile.

'By the Lord Harry, that's a good idea!' exclaimed Phelps. 'But how is it going to be done?'

'I'll tell you,' said Mr. Leeming complacently, and proceeded to do so with a great wealth of detail.

11

Syd the Piper

Mr. Sydney Higgins searched the pockets of his threadbare suit and gazed gloomily at the meagre result in the palm of his none-too-clean hand. Two pennies, a French halfpenny, a battered sixpence, and a shilling represented his entire capital. It was not an inspiring sum, and his low forehead wrinkled in a frown of disgust.

Something would have to be done, and 'something', in Mr. Higgins's limited vocabulary, meant another 'job'. The last had been none too profitable. The necklace, which he had with much trouble and labour succeeded in removing from Lady Clinmore's bedroom had been worth all of £2,000, but old Baumstein had beaten him down to £50. He was a notoriously mean old devil, even for a 'fence', but he had the reputation of being safe, which was a consideration.

Mr. Higgins lowered his skinny form into the chair by the rickety table and despondently turned his attention to the unappetising breakfast, which his shrewish landlady had brought him. He was a skilful larcenist, and was known to the police and his fellow artists as Syd the Piper, from his habit of entering houses by climbing the waste pipes to an upper window.

He was still considering when the stout landlady announced the visitor.

'Good morning!' said the well-dressed man who came into the shabby little bed sitting room. 'Your name is Higgins?'

Mr. Higgins was slightly alarmed. The man didn't look like a 'busy' but you never could tell these days, what with police colleges and things.

'Supposin' it is, then what?' he demanded noncommittally.

The visitor smiled at his evident uneasiness.

'There is no need to be afraid,' he said easily. 'I am not connected with the police. I have merely come to put a proposition to you which I think you will find profitable.'

Mr. Higgins was by no means reassured. All the suspiciousness of his class came uppermost.

'What you talkin' about?' he muttered. 'Who are you?'

'Who I am doesn't matter,' answered the other. 'If you wish to call me any thing you can call me Mr. Smith. That's as good a name as my own. What I've come for is to ask if you are prepared to earn a hundred pounds for a very simple job?'

Mr. Higgins' small eyes narrowed.

'Tell us wot it is,' he answered cautiously.

The visitor sat down opposite to him.

'All I want you to do,' he said, 'is to break into a certain house at one o'clock next Thursday night. You will make your way to the study — which you will find easily because you will be provided with a plan — and you will proceed to thoroughly ransack the place. You will strew papers about and generally give the place the appearance of being burgled, but you will actually take nothing. You will then go. For that I am prepared to give you a hundred pounds — fifty now and fifty when you have completed your job. What do you say?'

Mr. Higgins could say nothing. Amazement held him dumb. He stared at the man before him with his loose mouth hung open.

'Yer don't want me to take nothin'?' he managed to gasp at last. 'Wot's the idea?'

'That's my business,' was the curt reply. 'I've told you what I want done. You can either accept or refuse just as you like.'

Mr. Higgins hesitated, and was lost.

'Awlright, guv'nor,' he said. 'It's a bet.'

'Good!' The man before him nodded and tossed a bundle of notes on to the table. 'You'll find fifty there. Now listen carefully while I give you detailed instructions.'

Mr. Higgins picked up the notes with great alacrity, counted them and stowed them away in his pocket.

'I'm listenin', guv'nor,' he said, and adopted an attitude of strained attention.

The visitor spoke slowly and carefully, making sure that his audience understood every word, and even getting him to repeat certain portions of his instructions.

At that precise moment, the Angel, unconscious of the plot that was being hatched against her, was puzzling over the photograph of Uncle Ebenezer and trying to discover the reason for its tremendous attraction for the unknown. True to his promise, he had rung up on the following day and suggested that she should meet him in Hyde Park near the bandstand at eight o'clock the same evening, bringing the picture with her. Her answer had been a curt refusal, and she had cut off in the middle of his string of threats.

She was still examining the aged souvenir when Cordelia came in with her morning coffee.

'How's Brother Bert?' inquired the Angel. 'Have you been over to see?'

The maid nodded.

' 'E don't 'alf look a sketch,' she answered. 'With 'is face all over black oil an' grease. You wouldn't reckernise 'im.'

'That was an idea,' said her mistress. 'I

hope Harker will find him useful.'

'If 'e do it'll be the first time Bert's bin useful ter anybody,' remarked Cordelia, with a sniff. 'Any'ow, 'e's makin' 'im work, an' that's somethin' 'e ain't ever done before. 'E said 'e 'ad an easier time at Pentonville.'

Angela laughed.

'He's lucky not to be back there,' she said. 'But I don't think anyone will think of looking for him at the garage. I shouldn't go over too often if I were you.'

'Me! I don't want ter go at all,' said Cordelia. 'That there Ginger is allus tryin' ter get fresh. I don't mind that sort o' thing with somebody me own class, but not anybody like him.'

'Which reminds me,' said the Angel. 'Who was that very respectable man I saw you with yesterday? Looked rather like a retired bishop — if bishops ever do retire.'

Cordelia's small cheeky face reddened.

'Oh, 'im,' she answered, fingering her apron nervously. 'Now 'e is class if you like. Such a nice feller, an' speaks beautiful. I met 'im in the pictures — '

'I thought he was your father,' said the

Angel innocently and untruthfully. Cordelia bridled.

' 'E's not so old,' she said defensively, 'round about fifty, I should say, when a man's in 'is prime: I ain't got no time fer these bits o' boys what buys you a twopenny bar of choc'late an' thinks you're theirs for life.'

'I see you speak from experience,' remarked Angela.

'An' I've 'ad some, too,' said Cordelia. 'If I was to tell you — '

'Don't,' said the Angel hastily. 'Leave me still believing in the innocence of my fellow-creatures. What's the name of this rare paragon or didn't he tell you his name?'

'Oh, yes, we properly introduced ourselves,' said Cordelia. 'Everything was open an' above board, as you might say. 'Is name's Limpet, an' 'is Christian name's Octavius.'

'How romantic,' said Angela. The name conveyed nothing to her except that she thought it was peculiar, for she was quite unaware that Jimmy Holland even possessed a servant, and could not appreciate the irony of a fate that had made acquainted the sister of an escaped convict and the manservant of an officer of high rank in the very force that was bending all its endeavours to find him. One day she was to bless the providence that had brought those two together, for it was to be the means of saving her life.

12

The Frame-Up

Following a grey and chilly day, that Thursday evening developed a thin mist that was half drizzle and half fog. The man who had been detailed to keep watch on the Angel turned up the collar of his coat and eyed the half-invisible block of flats in which she lived, gloomily and a little resentfully. He had just taken over from his brother detective and was not looking forward to his long vigil.

Angela Kesson was at home — he had discovered that from his companion before he had departed — and she looked like stopping there. A big black saloon drew noiselessly up, and a man got out and entered the vestibule. The detective moved idly away to the end of the street. and as he reached it the man knocked at the door of the Angel's flat.

Angela was reading when Cordelia

burst excitedly into the sitting room.

'The police is 'ere again.' She whispered dramatically. ' 'E's in the 'all.'

'Inspector Holland?' said the Angel.

'No, another feller,' said the maid.

'I'll see what he wants.' The girl went out into the little hall and found a big, thickset man waiting by the door.

'I'm sorry to trouble you, miss,' he said respectfully. 'But I've been asked to take you to the Yard.'

'Do you mean arrest me?' asked Angela.

'No, miss. They want to ask you some questions — about Mr. Webb. I've got a car waiting miss, and I was told they wouldn't keep you long.'

The Angel considered: She could scarcely refuse and she would like to see the inside of the grim building, which she had passed so often.

'Will you wait while I put on a coat?' she said, and he nodded. She was back dressed for the street in five minutes, during which she had explained the circumstances to a scared and suspicious Cordelia.

'They're goin' ter pinch yer — you mark my words,' prophesied the maid darkly.

'Don't be silly!' said the Angel, and went to meet her escort.

'This way, miss,' he said, as they reached the vestibule, and led her across a strip of shiny pavement to a big car that was waiting. He opened the door and she stepped in. As the door closed she saw a dim figure huddled in the seat, and instinctively a warning of danger came to her. She turned, but hands gripped her roughly and pulled her down. Something pricked her arm sharply, and her senses swam . . .

★   ★   ★

Mr. Syd Higgins sat in the car drawn up by the kerb in the deserted side street and felt qualms of misgivings in his heart. His companion in the opposite corner had not spoken for some time, and he might have fallen asleep if the glow from his cigar had not testified otherwise. They seemed to have been waiting there hours, and Mr. Higgins was feeling fidgety and impatient. The proposition that had seemed so alluring in his little bed-sitting room took on a different aspect the more he thought about it.

'Wot's the time?' he ventured presently. 'Ain't it gettin' near?'

The man in the corner stirred. There was a little flicker of light, and the face of a gold wristwatch appeared vividly in the darkness and disappeared again as the lighter was flicked out.

'Half an hour yet!' came the laconic reply.

Mr. Higgins grunted.

''Ave we only been 'ere twenty minutes?' he said. 'Blimey, it seems hours!'

The other man said nothing, and Mr. Higgins moved uneasily.

He leaned forward suddenly. The lights of a car had appeared at the end of the little street, and as they came nearer they drew into the side and stopped a few yards away.

'Stay where you are!' warned Daniel Phelps, and, opening the door, got out. He walked towards the other car, and the curious Mr. Higgins, peering through the window, saw him stop and talk to somebody within. After a little while he came back. 'You'd better get started, now,' he said, and reluctantly Mr. Higgins ascended on to the wet and shining pavement.

* * *

Angela Kesson came out of a pit of impenetrable blackness with throbbing temples and a dry mouth. She could feel a queer vibration and sense of motion, and after a second or two's hazy speculation, remembered. She was in the car, which had come to take her to Scotland Yard. Of course, that had been a trick. The prick in her arm and the sudden faintness had been due to a drug. She kept very still as her brain rapidly cleared. Where was she being taken to, and who was responsible?

Cautiously she opened her eyes a fraction, so that she could see through her long lashes, but it was very dark; too dark to distinguish anything clearly. Was this another move on the part of the unknown who was after the photograph? There was certainly a man huddled in the other corner — she could just make out his dim outline — but who he was, it was impossible to tell. She came to the conclusion that her wisest course would be to pretend that she was still under the influence of the drug and see what happened. It would give her a small advantage, and any advantage was a lot in the circumstances.

The car was still speeding through the night, and she wondered where it was making for — how long it would be before they reached their destination — wherever it was.

She was feeling better with every passing second. Her head still ached a little, but her senses were unclouded. There was one thing she possessed which might prove useful in an emergency. She still wore on her finger the ring which she had used with such good effect on Montgomery Webb — and it was recharged. The drug it contained was harmless, and its effects passed swiftly, but it might be sufficient to give her a start.

The car swung round a corner and slowed. She saw ahead two dim lights that were stationary, and then the machine in which she sat came to a halt. Had they come to the end of the journey? Neither the driver or the man in the corner appeared to have any intention of getting out. A figure came into view beside the window, and her companion let it down.

'That you, Leeming?' whispered a man's voice; and Angela's heart leapt. So the man in the car was Oscar Leeming! She had not expected that. It threw a different complexion on the reason for her abduction.

'Yes, I've got the girl,' replied Mr. Leeming. 'Is Higgins with you?'

'Waiting in the car,' was the reply. 'He may as well get busy now. I'll tell him. It'll take a little while to get into the house.'

The listening girl was puzzled. Who was Higgins? And what house was he supposed to 'get into'? And then Leeming made a remark that gave her the clue to the situation.

'She'll be clever if she gets out of this!' he said, with a chuckle.

'The drug ought to be wearing off soon. She should come round just about the time they find her in old Deeping's study and the place ransacked. Caught in the act, eh?'

'I said at the time it was a clever scheme!' grunted the other and now she recognised his voice. Daniel Phelps! And they were going to 'frame' her! That was to be their revenge for the way she had tricked them; the method they had evolved to render her harmless for the future.

Her brain worked rapidly. She only had the haziest idea of what the plan was, but her nimble wits filled in the blanks sufficiently to tell her roughly what was supposed to happen. The man Higgins would break into this house of old Deeping's, whoever he was, and set the stage for a burglary. Then she would be discovered in the dismantled study and the evidence would be complete. Unfortunately, they had misjudged the strength of the drug they had administered. That was a miscalculation that would bring about a different ending to the one that was expected

She waited, lying limply back, every sense alert. Phelps went away and Leeming closed the window. There was a long interval, and the man beside her began to move restlessly. Had something gone wrong, she wondered. She heard a hurried step, and saw Phelps at the window.

'It's all right,' he whispered excitedly, opening the door of the car. 'Higgins is back, and the door's open. Be quick!'

Leeming got out.

'He hasn't disturbed the household — ' he began.

'No, no! The way's clear for you. Hurry!' broke in Phelps excitedly.

'Help me get the girl out,' muttered Leeming, and leaned into the car.

The Angel felt hands seize her, and let her muscles relax. An idea had come to her which if she could carry it out — She was lifted out in Mr Leeming's strong arms.

'Have you got the tools and the mask?' asked Phelps.

'In my pocket,' breathed Leeming heavily. 'You're sure there's no chance of a patrolling policeman spotting me?'

'There's another half-hour before he's due,' answered Phelps. 'You ought to be through by then. I'll get along with Higgins.'

He hurried away, and Mr. Leeming carried his apparently unconscious burden up the street and round the corner into a wider road. A few yards away was an open gate, and into this he turned. Through her half-closed lids the Angel caught a glimpse of an imposing house standing in a strip of garden, and then Leeming had mounted a flight of shallow steps and slipped through a partly open door into a dark hall. Here he paused and set the girl down cautiously. It was the moment that the Angel had counted on and waited for. As he allowed his arms to slide away from her she contrived to press her ring against his hand. She heard him give a little exclamation, and smiled in the darkness. In a few seconds the drug would take effect.

He was fumbling in his pockets. The light of a torch wavered about the hall for a moment and went out. The Angel came noiselessly to her feet. Leeming was staggering now like a drunken man, and as she snatched the torch from his hand he collapsed in a crumpled heap. She flashed the light swiftly round, saw a grandfather clock against the wall and going over pulled at it with all her strength. It toppled and fell with a crash that was noisy enough to wake the dead.

The Angel was out of the front door before the echoes of that appalling din had died away, and, pulling it shut behind her, went swiftly down the short path to the gate. As she walked quickly up the wide thoroughfare she wondered what explanation Mr. Oscar Leeming would offer for being found in a strange house, with a mask and a set of burglar's tools in his pocket, and evidence of his nefarious intentions in a ransacked room upstairs. Whatever it was she was quite certain that nobody would believe him!

13

Miss Nobody from Nowhere

The magistrate eyed the dishevelled figure in the steel pen sternly.

'Have you anything to say?' he demanded; and Mr. Oscar Leeming, an unshaven and unprepossessing-looking man after his night in the cell, dazedly shook his head. 'Then I shall commit you for trial at the next assizes,' said the grey-faced magistrate tonelessly.

Mr. Leeming's horrified and scandalised lawyer, whom he had hurriedly summoned, rose hastily to his feet.

'On the question of bail, your worship — ' he began; but the magistrate shook his head.

'There can be no question of bail,' he declared emphatically. 'The police are under the impression that the prisoner is an exceedingly dangerous criminal, and strongly oppose such a thing. I must say I entirely agree with them.'

'My client has a complete answer to the charge brought against him your worship,' persisted the lawyer. 'His presence in Lord Deeping's house was accidental and entirely innocent, in spite of — '

'He will be able to offer a defence at his trial,' interrupted the magistrate. 'From the evidence brought by the police, which I have heard, I cannot agree with you that the prisoner's presence in Lord Deeping's house in the middle of the night was either accidental or innocent. There was a black silk mask found in his pocket, together with a complete set of burglarous implements of the latest pattern. Lord Deeping's study presented the appearance of having been thoroughly searched. And the fact that nothing was stolen does not mitigate the offence.'

The lawyer bowed and Mr. Leeming was taken back to his cell. Angela Kesson, seated in the well of the little police court, rose as the next case was called and made her way to the exit. She had come to see the result of the recoil of Mr. Leeming's cleverness against himself, and was satisfied.

The proceedings had been briefer than she had expected. Evidence of arrest had been given; a statement by the Hon. Freddie Babbington, Lord Deeping's son, concerning how he had been awakened by a loud noise, had gone to investigate, and found the prisoner in a dazed state by the side of an overturned clock in the hall, and telephoned for the police, was listened to, and that was practically all.

The Hon. Freddie had seen her, to his great surprise, and spent the rest of the time after he left the witness box debating what she was doing there, and how he could, with circumspection, make her acquaintance. When he saw her leaving he hurriedly made for the same exit, racking his brains for an excuse to speak. One of those accidents, which do occasionally occur at the psychological moment, gave him one.

The seats in that particular police court were set up on a raised dais. It was only a slight step — little more than four inches — but the Angel, in her hurry, failed to notice it. One of her high heels caught in the step, and she stumbled. There was nothing to save her, and she would have fallen heavily if Freddie had not jumped forward and caught her.

'Oh!' she exclaimed breathlessly, as she hung in his arms. 'I'm so sorry — I didn't notice the step! Thank you!'

'Luckily, I was near enough to catch you, Miss Kesson,' said Freddie Babbington; and she looked at him in surprise as she disengaged herself.

'You know me?' she asked.

'Unfortunately, no,' he replied — 'at least, I didn't, but I hope I do now — '

'Silence!' The voice of the usher interrupted him peremptorily.

'Come outside,' he whispered hurriedly. 'We seem to be annoying them.' He took her arm and led her out into the passage beyond the door. 'Now,' he went on, 'we can talk without danger of being arrested for contempt of court.'

'What have we got to talk about?' asked the Angel.

'Oh, anything,' replied Freddie vaguely. 'I've been wanting to talk to you ever since I saw you at the theatre with that old monstrosity. I was in the opposite box — '

'With Inspector Holland,' she broke in. 'I remember. So that's how you knew my name. Is Mr. Holland a friend of yours?'

'Went to school together,' said Freddie, his large face beaming at the unexpected stroke of luck that had come his way.

'Did he tell you anything else about me besides my name?' said the Angel; and he was instantly embarrassed.

'Well — er — he did say one or two things,' he stammered. 'But, of course, there's some mistake — '

He shifted uneasily, looked at her, looked at the little groups of people who were waiting about until their cases were called, and back again.

'Jimmy's an obstinate old devil,' he said at last. 'Good fellow — one of the best — but obstinate — always was. He's got a bee in his bonnet — '

'You do your friend an injustice,' said the Angel coolly. 'Obstinate he may be, but so far as I am concerned he has no bee in his bonnet. I advise you to heed his warning, Mr. Babbington. Goodbye!'

She was gone before the bewildered Freddie could gather his scattered wits and put the invitation that had been at the back of his mind.

She reached home to find an indignant and slightly apprehensive Cordelia hovering about the tiny hall.

'They're 'ere again,' whispered the maid hoarsely.

'Who?' demanded the Angel ungrammatically, loosening her fur.

'The perlice,' answered Cordelia, jerking her head towards the closed door of the sitting room.

'What, all of them?' said the Angel, her lips twitching.

'No, that feller wot came the other day — 'Olland,' replied Cordelia. 'I told 'im you was out, but 'e would wait — '

'It's my popularity,' remarked Angela, and twisting the handle, walked into the room.

Jimmy Holland, who was standing by the window, looking out, turned as she came in.

'I hope I'm not being a nuisance,' he began apologetically. 'But I wanted to see you rather particularly. You've been playing the fool for a long time. Unless you're sensible, you'll go on playing it once too often and find yourself in the hands of the police. I want to prevent that if I can.'

'You have strange ideas for a detective,' she remarked, with a smile.

'Possibly I have,' he replied. 'Until I had that interview with you the other day, I had even stranger ideas. I was under the impression that you were just a clever adventuress, out to get all you could, legally or otherwise. I don't mind admitting that I agreed with the general view at the Yard that you were one of the cleverest women thieves we'd ever come up against!'

'I'd no idea I was so notorious,' she said calmly. 'What made you change your mind?'

'You did!' said Jimmy Holland. 'I've met a good many female crooks since I joined the Police Force, and they run to type. You're not the type. And I haven't reached that conclusion because you're pretty but because I'm a sufficiently good policeman to detect the difference!'

She laughed — a little gurgling sound that thrilled him strangely.

'You're not real — you're like a detective out of a storybook!' she said. 'And have you come here just to tell me that?'

He looked at her steadily and nodded

'To tell you that and to warn you,' he replied. 'I don't know what idiotic reason you have for behaving as you do — you must have one, I suppose — but whatever it is, it's not worth the risks you're taking. Sooner or later you'll make a mistake, and then it will be too late. Even I shan't be able to help you then!'

For a fraction of a second her eyes softened, and then she laughed

'I shan't want anyone to help me,' she said. 'What I'm doing, I'm doing with my eyes open. Nobody knows better than I do the risks I'm taking. But I shall go on taking them until I have achieved my object.'

'Or landed yourself with a long term of imprisonment,' he put in.

'Yes, or that,' she answered coolly.

'What is your object?' he asked, after a moment's pause.

She threw the end of her cigarette into

the fire and watched it consumed with a little spurt of flame.

'That's my business,' she said; and his lips compressed.

'I'm sorry' he said simply. 'I hoped that you would tell me.'

She turned her face towards him.

'How do you know there is anything to tell?' she asked. 'Don't you think it's conceivable that perhaps you have made a mistake — that Scotland Yard is right, and that you are wrong?'

Jimmy Holland said nothing, but turned and picked up his hat

'Must you go?' asked the Angel, in exaggerated disappointment.

'There seems to be no point in my staying,' he said curtly. 'Goodbye!'

'Hadn't it better be au revoir?' she said sweetly. 'You're sure to be coming back, you know.'

'You'll be wise if you see that I don't have to!' he retorted, and walked to the door. On the threshold he paused and looked back.

'Who are you?' he asked suddenly; and she stared at him.

'Are you serious?' she said. 'Or is this another joke?'

'Quite serious!' he replied gravely. 'Who are you?'

'My name is Angela Kesson — you know that very well,' she said.

He shook his head.

'There is no such person as Angela Kesson,' he answered. 'All the records of such things have been searched both in this and other countries, and there is no record of such a person as Angela Kesson ever having been born.'

'Then I must be a ghost!' she said lightly; but her face was pale. 'How very — industrious — you have been, Inspector Holland!'

'I have been interested in you for a long time,' said Jimmy. 'Whose grave do you visit once a week in the little cemetery at Camberley?'

A faint sound escaped her lips, and now her face was ashen — dead white, with two great eyes that blazed angrily.

'You have interfered enough with my private affairs,' she whispered. 'I refuse to answer any of your questions!'

She looked so ill that Jimmy felt a wave of contrition come over him.

'I'm sorry,' he said penitently. 'I shouldn't have asked that!'

'You can go on asking — go on prying and probing. It's your business; you're paid for it. But you won't find out anything.' She recovered herself. 'If you're not satisfied with Angela Kesson, I'll give you another name!'

'What's that?' he asked.

'Miss Nobody from Nowhere,' she answered. 'Perhaps, after all, that's more appropriate!'

14

The Unknown Strikes

On a night shortly after her interview with Jimmy Holland, when the rain was descending in sheets and the shining streets were deserted, the Angel, clad in a tight-fitting raincoat and an oilskin hat, drove her little car out of Mr. Harker's garage and headed towards the City. She had no fear of being followed, for the watcher, to his relief, had been withdrawn. At that period the police were conducting a series of raids on suspected gaming houses in the West End, and every available man was required for this duty. Angela had made certain that the detective was no longer lurking in the vicinity of Wyvern Court before putting into operation the idea that had been maturing in her mind, and she came into the deserted region of Leadenhall Street without misgivings.

There was nobody in sight as she slowed down, and crawling along the sidewalk, peered through the blurred window of the car, seeking the narrow turning which she had previously noted as suitable for her purpose. She almost missed it even though she was looking for it, and had to run back in reverse before she could turn the car into the lane. High office buildings towered on either side as she ran the machine into the ill-lighted alley and brought it to a halt opposite a dark entry on her right. Getting out she switched off the headlights, and taking a key from her pocket crossed the strip of pavement and inserted it in the lock of the main door. It was stiff and difficult to turn, but she managed it after an effort, and pushed the door open. Slipping into the little passage beyond, she closed the door behind her, took out her tiny torch, and switched it on.

Before her was a flight of stairs leading upwards to the various offices into which the building had been divided. She had waited patiently for one of these to fall vacant, and had received the agreement constituting her the tenant on the morning of the day that had proved so unfortunate for Mr. Oscar Leeming. The two tiny rooms that she had succeeded in renting were on the top floor, but she made no effort to climb the gloomy stairs. She was not interested in her new acquisition, except inasmuch as it gave her the right of entry and a key to the main door.

Passing through to the back of the building, she produced another key, unlocked a second door, and found herself in a small, dirty yard. It was still raining heavily, a steady downpour that looked as if it was likely to continue for the rest of the night. The ray of her torch scarcely made any impression on the darkness, but it was sufficient to augment her memory.

The yard was divided from the next by a low wall, and this she climbed, dropping into another enclosed square of concrete that was as much like the first as two peas. She negotiated four walls in all before, a little breathless and very wet and grimy, she reached her objective. After a moment's pause to rest she found a door similar to the one in the block from which she had started, and flashed her light on the lock. It looked a fairly simple one, and taking a leather roll from her pocket, she selected a curious little steel instrument and worked silently. In a moment or two the door was open.

Gathering up her roll of tools, she entered the building, shut the door and made her way to the front. This time she began to ascend the stairs and mounted until she came to the third floor, where a door bearing the inscription 'Abel Scarthright' in black lettering on white painted glass told her she had reached her destination.

Again the leather roll appeared, and a diamond neatly cut a circle out of the glass. The Angel inserted a gloved hand, pulled back the catch, and the next second was inside the office.

It was not a very large room, but the furnishing was comfortable. She stood for a moment taking stock of its contents, and then going over to the big desk that occupied the centre began methodically to search it.

Drawer after drawer she opened and examined, but she failed to find what she was seeking. She did the same with the filing cabinet, but with like result. Mr. Scarthright's business was apparently completely open and above-board. She bit her lip in disappointment. His private house she had already searched. If there was nothing here — and then she saw the safe.

It was not very large, and a quick examination showed her that it was not very modern, either. Stripping off her coat, she knelt in front of it and began to work on the massive door, utilising all the skill that an expert safebreaker had patiently taught her. It took her an hour and a half to get the door open, and she went through the contents eagerly. Nothing!

Nothing, that is, that was of much use to her. There was a roll of money, which she put in her pocket without counting, but what she had hoped to find was not there. Perhaps Scarthright was clever enough to keep such dangerous things in a safe deposit or at his bank.

It was with a sense of disappointment that she eventually found herself at the door of the block from which she had set out.

Her car still stood where she had left it. She got in and pressed the starter with her foot. As the engine picked up and she reached towards the gear lever, a cold circle pressed suddenly in the back of her neck and a voice whispered menacingly:

'I thought you were never coming, Miss Kesson.'

The Angel went rigid, for the voice was the voice of the unknown who was so anxious to obtain possession of Uncle Ebenezer's photograph!

15

'Either, Or —'

'I'm afraid my unexpected presence has given you rather a shock!' went on the whispering voice behind the Angel. 'But I've been watching you all the evening, and this seemed to be too good an opportunity to miss.'

'You seem to have gone to a great deal of trouble,' retorted the Angel calmly. 'Can I drop you anywhere?'

She had recovered from the momentary fear, which that icy touch on her neck had induced.

'You can. You can take me exactly where I tell you!' he replied.

'I'm rather tired, and I'm going home,' she remarked. 'If you're going the same way — '

'I'm going the same way as you are,' he said. 'But, unfortunately, it's not to Wyvern Court. Unfortunately for you, I mean.'

'In that case, I think you'd better get out and walk,' she said; 'or, alternatively, try to find a taxi — '

'You're talking foolishly,' he interrupted curtly. 'You'll do as you're told, otherwise — ' The pistol pressed a trifle harder. 'Well, otherwise it may be unpleasant.'

'It's unpleasant, anyway!' she retorted. 'Please don't fidget about with that thing. It tickles!'

'It can do worse,' he replied meaningfully. 'You know what I want? I want that photograph, and this time I mean to have it.'

'Do you imagine that I carry it next to my heart?' asked the Angel.

'Wherever it is, you can get it,' he answered grimly; 'and if you want to save a lot of trouble for yourself, you will.'

'You certainly are a man with one idea,' she remarked. 'How long do we stop here? I'm rather wet, and very tired — '

'We'll go now,' he said. 'Back out of this lane and then follow my directions.' She obeyed, since for the moment at least there was nothing else to do, and the car glided smoothly out into the still deserted

131

stretch of Leadenhall Street.

'Now make for Staines!' ordered the unknown as she brought the machine to a halt and slid the lever out of reverse.

'I'd much rather go home,' answered the Angel. 'It's not the best night to choose for a joy ride, and — '

'You'll go to Staines,' he answered. 'And I can assure you that this is no joy ride.'

'I was beginning to think so myself,' she agreed calmly. 'As an hilarious companion you haven't exactly got everything. Perhaps you'll improve on acquaintance.'

'You will have ample opportunity for discovering that,' he retorted.

'Well, if you're determined to go to Staines, I suppose we'd better go,' said the Angel resignedly. 'What do we do when we get there? Turn round and come back again?'

She was beginning to enjoy herself. The threat of the pistol resting lightly against her back no longer disturbed her. The man dared not shoot: to kill her would, so far as he knew, put the photograph he was so anxious to obtain beyond his reach for ever. His only chance was to try to terrorise her into complying with his demands, and she refused to be terrorised. Equally, she had no intention of going to Staines. She was perfectly well aware of what awaited her there. The unknown's object was to keep her a prisoner somewhere until he had forced her to send for the photograph. She knew this as certainly as if he had said so in so many words; knew also that once they arrived at this unknown destination there were many ways and means by which he could achieve his object. The car was running along the Embankment when she put the idea that had occurred to her into execution. There was a coffee-stall at the corner of Northumberland Avenue, and as they passed it she saw that several people were standing under the shelter, eating and drinking. She made an almost imperceptible movement with her foot, and the steady hum of the engine changed, there was a jolt, and the car stopped.

'What are you doing? Why have you stopped?' snapped the man behind her harshly.

'I don't know — something seems to have gone wrong,' she replied, and, with a flick of her finger, jerked the ignition control lever on the wheel to full retard. 'Do you know anything about cars?'

She asked the question as casually as possible, though in his answer lay the whole success or failure of her scheme.

'No, nothing!' he snarled. 'Can't you make it go?'

'I'll try!'

She pressed the starter and the motor whined, but the engine, although it spluttered and coughed, failed to pick up. It would have been a miracle if it had, with the ignition lever in the position it was, as she very well knew. Again and again she tried, recklessly exhausting her batteries, but without success.

'I'm afraid it's no good,' she said smoothly. 'She seems to be stuck.'

'Try the thing again,' he interrupted, and she complied.

'I'm afraid it's no good,' she said, when this attempt had been equally futile. 'We shall have to postpone our little trip until another time.'

He was disconcerted, and she knew it. He muttered something below his breath, and moved uneasily. 'This is a lucky accident for you,' he began, and stopped with an exclamation. The Angel looked round, saw the majestic figure that was crossing the road under the glare of the light standards and realised why. She heard the door click, and, turning, found her companion had slipped out on the other side.

'I'll see you again!' he snarled and was gone.

It was nearly four when she reached her flat, tired and cold, but thankful that her second meeting with the unknown had ended so satisfactorily. Luckily for her peace of mind she could not foresee the result of the third. If she had, even her courage might have failed before the ordeal that was in store.

16

The Cross Without a Name

In spite of Jimmy Holland's resentment at the Angel's reception of his friendly visit, he found it impossible to feel any animosity against her.

He told himself that his interest was purely academic. That here was a girl who represented a mystery, and that since it was his job to solve mysteries, he must naturally allot her a certain amount of attention in the course of his working day. That he was giving to her far more thought and attention than this conclusion warranted never occurred to him.

His first meeting with Angela Kesson had caused him to reconsider all the views he had previously held concerning her, and his second had confirmed him in his opinion that she was no ordinary adventuress. Jimmy prided himself on a knowledge of human nature, and was entitled to trust in his judgment considering the number of times he had proved himself right. And his judgment told him that the Angel was not a crook. That the things that had been attributed to her were true he was not prepared to deny, but that there was some mystery other than the obvious one he was certain. There was a mystery surrounding this girl and her actions that was very intriguing, and he was determined to discover what it was.

He took his first step towards the fulfilment of this project on the morning of the day following the Angel's excursion to Leadenhall Street. His long open racing car carried him to Camberley and set him down at the gate of the little church. Here, if anywhere, there should be a clue to the mystery he was trying to solve. He had not forgotten the result of his remark concerning that weekly visit of hers to the tiny cemetery — yes, if anywhere, there should be a clue here. The watcher had made his report in detail, and Jimmy had no difficulty in finding the grave. He stood bare-headed gazing down at the neat little mound with its sheaf of blood-red roses beginning to fade and crushed by the rain. Who lay under them? A relative — a friend — a husband? There was no inscription on the plain cross at the head — no tablet to show whose grave this was. But it ought not to be difficult to find out. Probably the sexton would know. Jimmy made his way back to the church and was lucky, for as he neared the doors a man in a black cassock came out.

'Good morning,' Jimmy greeted him pleasantly. 'Can you tell me where I can find the sexton?'

'You won't 'ave to go far, sir,' said the man, with a smile. 'I'm the sexton.'

'I'm fortunate,' said Jimmy. 'I want to make an inquiry concerning one of the graves. It's in the other part of the cemetery, and it has a stone cross but no name on it. Can you tell me whose it is?'

The good-humoured face before him changed. The smile faded and was replaced by a scowl.

'Look 'ere, what's the game?' demanded the sexton angrily.

138

Jimmy regarded him in astonishment.

'There's no game so far as I am aware,' he retorted curtly. 'I merely asked a civil question — '

'An' how many more of yer are there?' snapped the man. 'Are you doing this for a bet or something?'

'I really don't know what you mean,' protested Jimmy. 'Am I doing what for a bet?'

'Puttin' all these questions about that there grave,' said the sexton. 'See here, mister, go an' ask your friends. They'll tell you what you wants to know.'

He began to move away, but Jimmy caught his arm.

'Listen, my friend,' he said quietly, 'you seem to be under a wrong impression. If other people have been making the same inquiries I have no knowledge of them.'

The man looked at him doubtfully.

'I'm sorry if I've been 'asty,' he muttered, 'but I began to think it was some kind o' joke.'

'That's all right,' Jimmy waved aside the half-hearted apology. 'How many people have asked the same question?'

139

'Two,' answered the sexton. 'There was a man 'ere yesterday mornin' and another in the afternoon, and when you came this mornin', well, you can't blame me for gittin' cross-like. I thought it was a joke.'

'I'm not blaming you,' said Jimmy, frowning. 'What were these men like?'

The sexton was vague. They were well-to-do — one had come in an expensive car — and they were both middle-aged. Beyond that he was not helpful.

Jimmy pursed his lips. Who were these men who were making inquiries along the same lines as himself? Not connected with the police, that was certain.

'I told 'em what they wanted to know,' said the red-faced sexton. 'An' I thought it queer that two people should ask the same thing within a few hours of each other. Then, when you come along — '

He was apologetic, redundantly so.

'Well, let's get back to our original question,' said Jimmy, cutting him short. 'Who is buried in that grave?'

'A lady called Mrs. Smith,' answered the man. 'She used to live in the village with her daughter.'

Jimmy's surprise showed in his face.

'Mrs. Smith?' he echoed.

'That's right, sir,' the sexton nodded. 'Not what you'd call a very uncommon name, is it?'

'No.' The young inspector shook his head. 'When did she die?'

The sexton wrinkled his forehead.

'Must be about five years ago,' he answered, after a long effort of memory. 'Yes, quite that, sir. She died soon after they came to live 'ere.'

'And she had a daughter?' asked Jimmy.

'Yes sir,' replied the sexton. 'Very pretty girl, too. You can often see 'er 'ere tendin' 'er mother's grave, though after 'er death she went to live in London — the daughter, I mean.'

So Angela Kesson's real name was Smith, thought Jimmy. Why had she changed it? Because it was too ordinary, or for some other reason? Or was Smith an alias, too?

'Where did they come from — Mrs. Smith and her daughter?' he asked, and the sexton looked surprised until he explained what he meant.

'Oh, I see, sir!' He shook his head. 'Well, I don't rightly know. Maybe Mrs. Bodkin 'ud be able to tell you that. She used to do for 'em.'

Jimmy obtained the address of Mrs. Bodkin, and leaving the delighted sexton staring at a ten-shilling note, set off to find her.

Camberley was a very small village, situated sufficiently far from any main road to have remained unspoiled — though there were signs that this would not be for long — and he had no difficulty in finding the house of the woman who had 'done' for Mrs. Smith and her daughter. It was a small cottage near the end of the High Street, and Jimmy introduced himself to the buxom, elderly woman who opened the door to his knock.

'Yes, I remembers 'er well, sir,' she said, nodding her grey head briskly and surveying him with very bright and very curious eyes. 'They 'ad the little cottage up by the green, an' I used to go twice a week to clean up for 'em. The poor lady died six months after they came 'ere, an' 'er daughter was terrible cut up. Something shocking the way she carried on, poor dear, an' one of the loveliest girls I ever see, too. She only stayed two months after 'er mother was buried, an' then she went to live in London, though I've bin told she comes regular to bring flowers for the grave.'

From lack of breath, Mrs. Bodkin paused, and Jimmy seized the opportunity to put a further question.

'No, sir, I can't tell you where they came from,' said the woman, 'an' they never mentioned nothin', neither. I did think it was curious, as they was real gentlefolk, if you know what I mean, and it seemed queer-like to me that they should have suddenly come to live in old Marden's cottage out of nowhere as you might say.'

Vividly there came to Jimmy's mind the phrase that the Angel herself had used — 'Miss Nobody from Nowhere.' She had said it was appropriate, and he was beginning to agree with her. There was little doubt, he thought, that 'Smith' was an alias. But if Smith was an alias, and there was no such person as Angela Kesson, who was the Angel?

Jimmy Holland drove back to London with a furrowed brow and a puzzled face. The Angel had supplied him with the greatest enigma he had come up against since he joined the Police Force.

17

An Interrupted Meeting

The arrest of Mr. Oscar Leeming on a charge of housebreaking caused a sensation; all the more so since he was known to have been a friend of Montgomery Webb, the mystery of whose murder was still unsolved. It was remembered that burglary had also figured prominently in that crime, and rumours began to spread rapidly to the effect that Leeming was also responsible for this and the murder of his friend. Naturally, neither the police nor the newspapers contributed even a hint towards such a conclusion; the man was still awaiting trial, and British justice is eminently fair, but the general public were less reticent. The possibility was openly discussed in clubs and in trains, in saloon bars and at street corners, with disastrous results to Mr. Leeming's moral character. These rumours reached the ears of that unfortunate man's worried lawyer and caused him considerable anxiety.

'There's not the slightest doubt that you're in a very awkward position,' he said, during one of his many interviews with his client. 'An extremely awkward position. You knew this man Webb intimately, and — Well, it's an awkward position.'

'You've said that three times, and I knew it before,' growled Mr. Leeming. 'It's altogether preposterous that such an idea should be spread abroad. Why should I want to kill Webb? We were the best of friends — '

'I'm not saying you killed him!' broke in the grey-haired solicitor. 'I'm only saying that people are suggesting you did, and I'm afraid that the police may hold a similar theory, which is going to be a very awkward — '

'Then what can be done?' demanded Mr. Leeming anxiously. 'Damn it, man, we must do something! They can't imprison me for something I'm not guilty of.'

'It may be worse than imprisonment,'

said the lawyer dispassionately, 'if they make out a case of murder against you.'

Mr. Leeming's flabby face went grey.

'You don't really think they're likely to do that, do you?' he said huskily. 'My heavens, it's dreadful — dreadful, Pell. You must do something — '

'I'll do my best, Leeming. You can be sure of that,' said Mr. Pell, but his tone was not encouraging. 'So far as I can see, all we can do is to engage a clever counsel, lay our cards on the table and hope for the best.'

On this unsatisfactory note the interview terminated.

While the stout and misguided Mr. Leeming languished in his uncomfortable cell, Daniel Phelps, Abel Scarthright and the rest of his associates held an uneasy meeting in the private room at the Holborn Restaurant, where the plot against the Angel's liberty had first seen the light of day.

'That girl's clever and dangerous!' grunted Jonathan Bellman round a big cigar. 'She's landed poor Leeming in the soup, and I think he'll have a devil of a job getting out of it.'

'It was Leeming's scheme, and he must bear the brunt of it,' said Abel Scarthright callously. 'You're right about that girl being clever and dangerous, Bellman. My office was broken into the night before last.'

Every head in the room turned towards him.

'You don't keep anything there — ' began Hathaway quickly, and Scarthright shook his head.

'No, I'm not like Webb; I'm satisfied to play safe. The profit's good enough for me from the syndicate.'

'How do you know it was the girl who broke in?' asked Phelps. 'Was anything stolen?'

'A little money, but that wasn't the object,' answered Scarthright. 'The safe had been opened and the whole place searched. I found two golden hairs on my desk — it was the Angel all right.'

Julian Hathaway flicked the ash from his cigar.

'I wonder who the devil she is, and what she's after?' he muttered thoughtfully.

'The point is,' put in Bellman slowly, 'that it doesn't matter whether she's a common thief or something else. She might be dangerous, and I think she ought to be stopped.'

'I agree with you,' said Scarthright quickly.

'How are we going to do it?' demanded Hathaway. 'Leeming tried and — '

'The whole trouble with Leeming's scheme was that it was too complicated,' interrupted Scarthright. 'There's a better and much simpler way in my opinion.' He looked significantly at the three men before him.

'I don't hold with violence.' Hathaway shook his head.

'You were always squeamish,' said Scarthright contemptuously. 'Listen to me.' He leaned forward and ground out the end of his cigar in the ashtray. 'We've got to look after ourselves; we don't know what game this girl is playing. She may, as Hathaway suggests, be just an ordinary thief, but she may not. We can't afford to take the risk. Without making any bones about it, we're engaged in organised blackmail on a big scale. It's been very profitable, thanks to the cleverness of our unknown president, and I hope it will continue to be so; but this girl may prove a very big source of danger. She may, for all we know to the contrary, be related to someone whom we've fleeced. Personally, that's what I believe, because you've got to remember that she's concentrated all her attention on our little group. If she was just a plain crook she would not have done that. So I say that, whatever steps we take — whatever steps — are justified.'

There was a silence when he had finished speaking.

'I suppose you're right, Abel,' said Phelps at last. 'What do you propose we should do then?'

'I propose to take drastic action,' answered Scarthright promptly. 'I propose that we eliminate the source of danger, and at once.'

'Are you suggesting murder?' asked Bellman bluntly.

'There's no other certain way, is there?' said Scarthright.

Hathaway moved uneasily in his chair.

'It's a risk,' he muttered. 'We've always drawn the line at anything like that — '

'Because we've never been up against the necessity,' broke in Scarthright. 'Now we are, and we've got to use emergency methods.'

Jonathan Bellman removed the cigar from his lips and blew out a cone of smoke. 'Have you any suggestion as to how it should be done?' he inquired unemotionally.

Scarthright shook his head.

'No,' he admitted; 'but it shouldn't be difficult — '

'Perhaps,' interrupted a musical voice gently, 'I can help you?'

Scarthright uttered a startled oath and sprang to his feet, turning in the same movement to face the slim, beautifully dressed lady that stood surveying him calmly, a hint of mockery in her grey eyes.

It was the Angel!

18

Drastic Action

Her eyes danced and her lips twitched with amusement as she saw the consternation that her sudden appearance had evoked.

'You're surprised to see me?' she remarked, with a dazzling smile. 'Please, don't trouble to offer me a chair, Mr. Scarthright. I'm not staying very long.'

'How — how did you get here?' Daniel Phelps found his voice and put the question.

'On my feet,' she replied calmly. 'I've been here quite a long time — behind that screen.' She nodded to a tall screen of faded red baize that stood in a corner by the door.

'Do you mean' — and Scarthright swallowed hard — 'do you mean that you've been listening?'

'Yes,' she answered. 'It was most

interesting. I was a little bored at first, but it got much more interesting after. But don't let me interrupt you — '

'How long have you been here?' demanded Bellman roughly.

She looked towards him and pursed her red lips.

'I'm afraid I'm not much good at estimating times,' she said. 'I slipped in when the waiter brought the coffee. It was really quite easy. Nobody saw me. For desperate conspirators you're rather lax, you know.'

Scarthright breathed hard through his nose. The voice, clear and musical as a bell, flicked like the thin lash of a whip.

'It's really very nice to see you all again,' went on the Angel. 'And so much nicer to see you all together instead of singly. You're so apt to get sentimental alone. It's because you're all so soft-hearted, I suppose. Isn't it a pity poor Mr. Leeming isn't here? — so charming and so naïve. I thought he was looking very queer when I saw him last, so perhaps a nice long rest will do him good — '

'We can very well dispense with this

fooling,' said Scarthright smoothly. 'Since you heard what we were discussing it seems a little futile.'

Angela lifted her shoulders a fraction of an inch and pouted.

'I think you're very unkind,' she said sadly. 'Quite a lot of girls would have been really cross if they'd overheard plans for murdering them. Because I'm broad-minded you don't like it.'

'On the contrary, I'm glad you are treating this situation so — er — sensibly,' retorted Scarthright grimly. 'Though I feel that it would be even better if you treated it — seriously.'

'The trouble with all you big, strong, silent men is that you're so solemn,' said the Angel. 'Life is real — life is earnest — you miss such a lot of enjoyment with that outlook. You should cultivate a sense of humour and a carefree attitude, sing in your bath — '

'I believe the woman's mad,' grunted Bellman disgustedly. 'Listen Miss Kesson — or Smith — '

'I prefer Kesson — don't you?' said Angela. 'It's so much more refined.'

'It's immaterial to me!' he retorted. 'I don't suppose that either is your real name.' He stared at her pointedly, but she only smiled. 'What is material is this. For a long time you've been prying into our private affairs. You've made fools of us and searched our belongings. You killed Webb because he discovered you in the act of searching his study — '

'Oh, no!' interrupted the Angel. 'I would not like you to think that of me. I wouldn't have hurt a hair of Mr. Webb's head.'

'Well, that's as may be,' growled Bellman. 'He was bald, anyhow.'

'That's what I meant,' said Angela sweetly.

'You've done all these things,' continued the grey-haired man, ignoring her remark, 'and now you come eavesdropping at a private conference What's the reason? What's behind it?'

'As the principal person concerned, I think I was entitled to gatecrash in here,' replied the Angel coolly. 'If a girl can't discuss her own murder, what can she discuss?'

She knew she had them at a disadvantage and was revelling in the knowledge.

Scarthright, who had been frowning thoughtfully in silence, suddenly raised his head.

'If you would condescend to be serious for a moment,' he said sarcastically, 'we might get somewhere.'

'I'm afraid I can't spare any more time now,' said the Angel regretfully looking at her watch. 'There's a sale at Willingtons and they're absolutely giving things away. Perhaps when you've completed your plans we might have another little chat, and I could go over them with you and make suggestions. Give me a ring sometime — '

'Not quite so fast,' said Scarthright, and with a swift movement he slipped between her and the door. 'The plans you mention are completed.'

His eyes had gone cold and hard, but even then she did not realise her danger. It never occurred to her that these men would attempt anything in a public restaurant where there was help within call. But she had underestimated the cleverness of Abel Scarthright, whose keen brain had suddenly shown him how to turn her unexpected appearance to his own and his companions' advantage.

'I wish I had time to hear them — ' she began lightly, and that was as far as she got, for Scarthright sprang forward, caught her round the waist and clapped his other hand over her mouth.

'Quick, Phelps — Hathaway! Hold her!' he said breathlessly as she struggled violently in his grasp.

'Are you mad, Scarthright?' cried Julian Hathaway. 'What the hell — '

'Do as I tell you and be quick!' snapped Scarthright. 'She's as strong as a — ' He gave a gasp of pain as the Angel's teeth met in his hand, but he kept it pressed over her mouth. Phelps and Hathaway came to his assistance, with alarmed faces.

'You'll get us all arrested for this,' muttered Daniel Phelps uneasily.

'I shall, if you stop to argue,' snarled Scarthright, his face white with pain. 'Grip her legs, Hathaway, you fool! Don't stand there like a blasted dummy!'

Hathaway obeyed. He seized the Angel's slim, silk-clad ankles and held the threshing legs still, while Phelps caught her by the arms and dragged her hands down to her sides. Scarthright shifted his grip suddenly. His lean, strong fingers felt for and found the pulsing arteries in her neck that fed blood to her brain, and pressed cruelly. Her frantic struggles grew less and less as the pressure increased, and then suddenly she went limp. Scarthright loosed his fingers, and his breath escaped from between his teeth in a long sigh of relief.

'Lay her down gently,' he panted, wiping his scratched and bleeding hands with his handkerchief. 'She'll be unconscious for a few minutes anyhow, and that will be time enough.'

'Of all the crazy fools I think you're the craziest!' said Phelps. 'What do you think is going to happen now?'

'I can tell you,' said Bellman angrily. 'There'll be the devil of a row! She's only got to call the nearest policeman — '

'She'll call nobody,' broke in Scarthright impatiently. 'Don't you realize that

158

we shall never have another opportunity like this?'

'Of getting gaoled,' put in Hathaway shakily. 'I agree with you. Supposing a waiter walks in now —

Scarthright stopped him with a savage gesture.

'I tell you I know what I'm doing!' he snapped. 'The whole plan came to me while she was talking. Nobody will come here until we ring. That's the arrangement, you know that.'

'Yes, that's all very well,' grunted Phelps. 'But what are we going to do with her? We can't just walk out and leave her here to be found. They know us here. They know we engage this room periodically for business luncheons — '

'We're not going to leave her here,' said Scarthright. 'She's coming with us.'

They stared at him as though he had suddenly taken leave of his senses, as indeed they were prepared to believe he had.

'I see,' growled Daniel Phelps sarcastically. 'We just carry her down to the car and nobody asks any questions.'

'That's nearly right,' agreed Scarthright easily. 'But we don't carry her. She walks.'

Old Jonathan Bellman scowled at him.

'I suppose you do know what you're doing?' he said. 'Personally it looks to me as though we are going to get into serious trouble.'

'We shan't get into any trouble at all,' asserted Scarthright, with conviction. 'Give me that brandy.'

He took the bottle of liqueur brandy that Hathaway gave him and looked at it. It was half full, and he nodded. 'That should be enough,' he muttered, and, going over to the Angel, he knelt beside her. The others watched him curiously as he forced open her mouth and poured a portion of the neat spirit between her lips.

'What the devil are you playing at?' demanded Phelps. 'What are you trying to revive her for?'

Scarthright made no reply. He was too intent upon his task. The unconscious girl swallowed a mouthful of the brandy, and he repeated the dose. When half the contents of the bottle had been disposed of in this way, Bellman grunted.

'She'll be as tight as an owl if you give her any more,' he remarked, and Scarthright looked up.

'It's taken you a long time to see the idea,' he retorted. 'Of course she'll be tight. That's what I want her to be. We've nothing here to keep her unconscious, have we? And if we had, an unconscious girl would take a lot of explaining away. But a drunken woman is a different matter. People may be shocked, but they won't ask questions, and she won't be capable of saying anything for herself.'

Daniel Phelps drew a long breath.

'It's a stroke of genius, Scarthright,' he said admiringly.

'How are you going to explain her presence here at all?' demanded Hathaway, a little colour coming back into his cheeks, and his scared look fading.

'I shall mention to the head waiter that she's my secretary,' replied Scarthright. 'She came to bring me some important documents, and we gave her one or two glasses of brandy. Not being used to it, it affected her.'

'And when she leaves here?' inquired

Bellman. 'What then?'

'She won't be a source of anxiety to us any more,' answered Scarthright significantly. 'We'll take her straight to that old house of yours at Horsham, Phelps.'

'Ashley Lodge,' said Daniel Phelps, raising his eyebrows. 'It's in a terrible state of repair. I've been trying to sell it for months — '

'She won't be there long enough to worry about its condition,' retorted Scarthright. 'There's a well in the garden, isn't there? I remember you telling me once that there was.'

Phelps nodded slowly. He understood then what the Angel's fate was to be.

19

'Out of the Frying Pan —'

The Angel's eyelids flickered, and she moaned, moving restlessly, in a semi-dazed state. Presently she opened her eyes and stared vacantly into a diffused greyness that held no meaning. She felt horribly ill. Her eyes smarted and burned; her head throbbed violently as though thousands of miniature steam hammers were working overtime. Her mouth was dry, and there was a curious half sour, half acrid taste, which puzzled her. Anyone used to the unpleasant symptoms of the 'morning after the night before' would have accurately placed these distressing sensations and classified them under the single terse heading 'hangover'. But the Angel, who was abstemious in all things, took some time to correctly diagnose the reason for her condition.

She opened her eyes again, and for the second time tried to sit up.

The pain in her head was just as severe, but the dizziness was not. Gritting her teeth she succeeded, and discovered she was in a small room with a tiled floor indescribably dirty, and obviously the scullery of a fairly large house. There was a door facing the window, which she supposed led into the kitchen. After several attempts she managed to scramble to her feet and was instantly violently sick in the sink. The effect of this was to make her feel better, and it also gave her a clue to what had been the matter with her. So that's what they had done! While she had been unconscious they had made her drunk! And she was now getting sober. Whoever had thought of that deserved full credit. It was brilliant.

She steadied herself by the sink, and tried the taps. Nothing happened when she turned one. but the other supplied a trickle of water. It was reddish at first, but after a little while it ran clear. She bathed her face and felt refreshed She would have liked a drink, but concluded that the water probably came from a tank and was not fit. The fact that the warm tap was dry confirmed what the state of the place suggested, that the house was disused.

Where had she been brought to, she wondered, and with difficulty climbed on to the edge of the stone sink. It enabled her to reach the window and she peered out. All she could see was an expanse of weeds and rank grass and thickly growing trees. It looked as if she were somewhere in the country but that was not certain. What was certain was that she was in a very nasty position. These men, having got her, would undoubtedly make the most of this opportunity, and the most in this case meant that she would die just as soon as they were ready.

This was a foregone conclusion. With her own ears she had heard them decide to kill her, and unless she could prevent it they would do so. She took stock of her prison to see if there was any likelihood of her getting out. The window was impassable. The bars were thick and set closely together. She went over to the door. It was stout and solid, and apparently, locked on the outside. There seemed no possibility of escape by either means.

She found her handbag, philosophically took out her cigarette case and lighter, and, hoisting herself on top of the copper, lit a cigarette. It didn't taste very nice, and she made a grimace, but the smoke was soothing to her nerves, and she inhaled deeply. Her watch told her that it was a few minutes after six, which meant that she must have been unconscious for just over three hours — time enough, she thought, to have been taken a considerable distance.

She finished the cigarette, and pressed out the stub on the stone beside her. Although she was still feeling shaky and ill, her brain was clear, and she began to seek for a means of escape. There seemed to be no one in the house except herself, as she could hear no sound at all. Probably, after making sure that she was securely locked in, the men who had brought her to this place — wherever it was — had gone away until it got dark. Would they come back then to complete whatever they had in mind? Or was the intention to leave her where she was — to starve? She came to the conclusion that it was more likely that they would come back.

The light was fading rapidly from the sky. In a few more minutes it would be quite dark, and then they would come . . . She raised her head suddenly and listened. Had they come already? Was that a faint sound she had heard? It was not repeated, and she put it down to her imagination — that almost inaudible creak which had reached her ears — most likely it was the squeak of some animal outside. And then, as she once more turned her attention to the problem of escape, it came again louder, and this time, unmistakable — the creak of a raised window-sash. So they had returned.

She braced herself and turned to face the closed door, alert and ready for what might happen. There was still a chance that her wits might save her: that these men would make some false move of which she could take advantage.

She heard a footstep on bare boards. Somebody was crossing the floor of the

167

room beyond, and it was only a single footstep. There was, then, only one of them. The Angel glanced quickly round her in the gloom. If she could find some weapon and wait behind the door —

Her eyes fell on what she wanted — a dusty bottle, which stood under the sink — and, without making a sound, she went swiftly over and picked it up. It was a large stone bottle that, at one time, had contained ginger-beer; the faded label was that of a well-known firm of mineral water manufacturers. Gripping it by the neck, she took up her position near the door, and waited.

The footsteps had stopped, and there was silence. She pictured the person beyond that door listening, and kept as still as though she had become part of the room. If he was careless — if he came quickly through the door, as she hoped he would, there was yet a chance —

It seemed to her that years passed before the key rasped in the rusted lock and the door began to open slowly. She raised her weapon and waited tensely, her eyes fixed on the widening space between door and jamb. Presently, after an eternity, the door stood fully open and she caught a glimpse of the form in the oblong opening. But the man did not cross the threshold, as she had hoped he would, and on which the success of her hasty plan depended. Instead:

'Please move where I can see you,' said a voice. 'I have a pistol in my hand, and although I should not shoot to kill, I should have no hesitation in inflicting a painful wound.'

She nearly dropped the stone bottle in her surprise and astonishment, for the voice was the voice of none of the men she had expected. It was the husky muffled tones of the unknown seeker after Uncle Ebenezer's photograph.

20

The Houseboat

The Angel recovered quickly from the shock of that low, menacing voice, and moved out from beside the door.

'I have gone to a lot of trouble,' he said. 'I watched you enter the restaurant, and saw you leave with your escort. From your condition I guessed what had happened, and followed the car in which you were taken away.'

'Then you'll be able to tell me where I am,' remarked Angela. 'I'm very curious to know that.'

'You are in an old house on the outskirts of Horsham, which belongs to Daniel Phelps,' he replied. 'But we haven't time to talk further now. The gentlemen who brought you here will be coming back soon, and I have no desire that either you or I should be here when they do.'

'Our desires at the moment, then, are mutual,' said the Angel. 'Let's go!'

'Hold out your wrists!' he commanded; and, since there was no help for it, she dropped the bottle and obeyed. He reached forward, snapping on a pair of handcuffs, and she raised her eyebrows.

'Really, that was done most professionally!' she remarked, eyeing the manacles distastefully. 'You're not a policeman, by any chance, are you?'

'Never mind who or what I am!' he answered curtly. 'Come along, we'll take that journey to Staines which, unfortunately, we had to postpone the other night.'

He made a gesture with the barrel of the pistol he held, and she walked past him into the big kitchen.

'Through that door and along the passage,' he ordered close behind her. 'And I warn you, I shall certainly shoot if you try any tricks — and the result will be painful.'

A closed car, almost hidden by bushes, stood near the rotting gates of the old house, and to this he conducted her.

'Get in!' he said, opening the door, and when she was inside took his place beside her. She saw for the first time the muffled figure of another man sitting behind the wheel in front, and then the car moved forward.

The Angel settled back in the cushioned seat and closed her eyes. She had escaped one danger to land into another, from which she would require all her ingenuity to extricate herself. But nothing could be done at the moment, and she took advantage of the interim to relax both mind and body. She would need every atom of energy she could muster later when the crisis came, as she knew it would as soon as they reached Staines and their unknown destination.

It was quite dark when she woke from a refreshing sleep, feeling distinctly better for it. The car was still moving smoothly, and looking through the near side window, she caught a glimpse of trees and hedges as they sped past.

'Are we nearly there now?' she asked politely.

'Nearly,' was the curt answer.

'I'm glad of that,' said the Angel. 'I'm beginning to feel hungry. I hope your programme includes dinner.'

He made no reply, and, shifting into a less cramped position, she watched the ribbon of road ahead visible in the headlights beyond the broad back of the driver. Suddenly she laughed softly, and her companion turned his head towards her.

'What's amusing you?' he asked gruffly.

'I was just thinking what a shock Mr. Scarthright and his friends must have had when they came back and found I'd gone,' she said.

'I don't suppose they will find it very funny,' he retorted; 'and I can assure you, you won't, either, unless you do what I want.'

'What do you want?' she inquired.

'I want that photograph.'

'Oh dear!' she sighed. 'Are you going to start that all over again?'

'If you're getting tired of it,' he snapped, 'you have your remedy.'

Before she could reply, the car swung suddenly into a side turning, jolting violently over a rutted surface, ran a short distance, and turned again. The Angel saw a gleam of water, a mass of bushes and trees, and a sloping grassy bank.

'Is this the river?' she said, and the man in the corner nodded.

'This is the river,' he said, 'and this is where we get out.'

As he spoke the car stopped. The Angel, following him out on to the roadway, saw that they had reached a deserted stretch of what was evidently the towpath.

The unknown spoke a whispered word to the silent driver, and he drove on leaving them standing side by side in the darkness.

'Where do we go from here?' inquired Angela.

Without answering, he gripped her arm and led her to the edge of the bank. Among the reeds was a dark splash of shadow which, as they came nearer, revealed itself to be a small dinghy. Her companion pulled on the mooring-rope and drew the little boat close in to the bank.

'Get in!' he ordered.

'Oh well, of course, if you insist,' she said, as she stepped down into the swaying craft. 'I hope you know more about boats than you do about cars — '

'Sit down and keep quiet!' he snapped. When he had untied the mooring-rope, he got in beside her, unshipped a pair of sculls, and thrust them into the rowlocks. A couple of powerful strokes sent the tiny dinghy gliding out towards midstream. The Angel, sitting meekly in the stern, wondered where they were making for.

The boat was heading for a dense patch of blackness on the opposite bank — the shadow thrown by a tall clump of trees — and as they entered the fringe of this she was able to make out the vague outline of a building that to her surprise seemed to rise straight out of the water. The nose of the dinghy bumped softly against the flat side of this peculiar structure, and then she saw that it was a medium-sized houseboat. The masked man hastily shipped his sculls and caught an iron ring, fixed in the platform-like deck that extended a couple of yards beyond the main portion of the building.

'Get out,' he said.

The Angel rose wearily.

'I seem to have done nothing else but get in or get out the whole evening,' she said, pathetically. 'It's very tiring. I hope there isn't going to be any more of it.'

'There isn't,' he retorted curtly.

He tied up the dinghy skilfully when she had climbed out, and joined her on the flat wooden platform. Then, taking a key from his pocket, he unlocked a door at the end of the houseboat, and pushed her into the dark interior. The place smelt damp and musty.

He struck a match, and in the feeble glimmer she saw that they were standing in a low-ceilinged, cabin-like apartment, comfortably furnished, but dusty and neglected. There was a lamp on a table in the centre, and this he lighted.

'I've no doubt it's very nice here in the summer,' said the Angel. 'But at this time of the year I much prefer my flat — '

'You can go back to your flat as soon as that photograph is in my possession,' he said.

'Why are you so anxious?' she asked.

'Why are you so obstinate?' he retorted. 'The photograph is no good to you. Why don't you give it up and save a lot of trouble and unpleasantness?'

'Because I'm curious,' she replied. 'I want to know the secret of Uncle Ebenezer — '

'You never will!' He caught her by the arm. 'That photograph is mine, and its secret is mine, too. You will write a letter to your bank authorising them to hand the photograph to the bearer — '

She laughed in his face — a musical ripple of sheer amusement.

'Do you really think I'm likely to do that?' she said.

'I know you'll do it' — his voice was hoarse — 'because the alternative will be so exceedingly painful that you will agree to anything to avoid it.'

21

Cordelia Seeks Advice

'Coo!' said Miss Cordelia Smith rapturously. 'This is a bit of awlright, this is.' She helped herself to a third éclair and smiled across the tea table at her escort. Mr. Limpet returned the smile benevolently.

'It gives me great pleasure to see you enjoying yourself, Miss Delia,' he remarked in his slow, stately manner. 'Perhaps, however you will forgive me if I point out that 'coo' is hardly the correct expression for a lady to signify delight, nor, if I may say so, is 'a bit of awlright' de rigueur in the best circles.'

'Wot's wrong with it?' demanded Miss Smith with difficulty, her mouth full of pastry.

'I would suggest,' said Limpet, 'that possibly 'This is really charming', or 'This is delightful', might be more suitable.'

Cordelia's round, black eyes surveyed him with astonishment.

'Well, wot I said means the same thing, don't it?' she remarked with a certain amount of truth.

'Oh, undoubtedly!' agreed Limpet, inclining his head. 'But I was merely showing you how the same sentiment could be more happily phrased.'

Cordelia's small face crinkled with laughter.

'You ain't 'alf a funny one,' she said. 'I could die laughing at some of the things you ses.'

Mr. Limpet's expression was a little pained as he sipped delicately at his second cup of tea.

'You're different to most fellers,' said Cordelia. 'There ain't no sloppy nonsense about you. You don't try any 'oldin' and kissin'.'

'I trust,' said Mr. Limpet, 'that I know how to behave myself.'

'Not that I ain't partial to a bit of romance,' went on Cordelia. 'But it 'as to be the right person, if you know wot I mean.'

'Exactly,' agreed Mr. Limpet. 'That is precisely my own view.' He glanced at his watch. 'Dear me,' he continued, 'how quickly the time has passed. I'm afraid, Miss Delia, that I shall have to be going. It is nearly six, and I must be back by six.'

He signalled to a waitress, collected the bill, and rose.

'I hope,' he said, as they left the little tea shop, 'that you will honour me with your company next Wednesday.'

'If you'd reely like me to,' she murmured coyly.

'Then we will meet at the usual place at three o'clock,' said Mr. Limpet. 'There is, I believe, a very excellent picture featuring Garie Hooper — '

'Oh, yes, I've bin dyin' ter see that!' exclaimed Cordelia rapturously. ' 'Panting Flames', Mona Languish is in it too; she ought ter be lovely.'

Mr. Limpet agreed, aplogised owing to the lateness of the hour for not seeing her home, and took his dignified departure. Miss Cordelia Smith walked back to Wyvern Court in a mental state that was bordering on ecstasy, so engrossed in her romantic dreams, that she became a source of great irritation to the hurrying throng whose thoughts were centred on the more prosaic problem of catching their various means of transport to their homes. She was surprised to find her mistress out when she reached the flat, for the Angel had definitely expressed her intention of spending the afternoon and evening at home, but she concluded that something must have happened to make her alter her plans, and went about her duties without thinking much more about it.

It was not until dinner time came and went without any word or message that she began to feel worried. Her mistress never stopped away without letting her know, and she wondered what could have happened. Her first thought was, that at last her ever-present fears had been realised and that the Angel had been arrested, but when she considered this dire possibility more thoroughly, it occurred to her that if such a thing had happened, she would have heard. The first thing the Angel would do would be to let her know.

But perhaps there had not yet been time for that. She waited in an agony of apprehension and uneasiness, but nine o'clock passed, and there was no message. A sudden idea came to her and, picking up the telephone, she called Mr. Harker's number. He answered her himself, and she put her question.

'No, Miss Kesson's car is here,' he said. 'She did come for it this morning, but we was puttin' two new tyres on, and she said it didn't matter as she'd go by taxi.'

'D'you know where she went?' asked Cordelia.

'No, I don't,' replied Mr. Harker, 'but maybe Ginger 'ull know. 'E got the cab for 'er — hold on a minute!'

He went away, and Cordelia waited impatiently. After what seemed to her to be hours, but was really only three minutes, she heard his voice again.

'Ginger says Miss Kesson told the driver to go to the 'Olborn Restaurant,' he said.

'Wot time was that?' demanded the worried maid.

'Oh, it 'ud be early!' replied Mr.

Harker. 'Let me see now, about 'alf-past twelve or a quarter to one. What's the matter?' he added anxiously. 'Nothing ain't 'appened to Miss Kesson, 'as it?'

'No!' snapped Cordelia. 'Only she ain't come 'ome yet, an' I was wonderin' where she was, that's all.'

She rang off and helped herself to a cigarette. Had anything happened, or was she just worrying herself unnecessarily? She didn't want to tell old Harker too much. He was a nosy old devil. There was an element of jealousy in this although she was unconscious of it. With the cigarette drooping between her lips she paced up and down, her eyes constantly turning towards the clock. Ten — half-past, and still no sign of the Angel.

There was something wrong. If she had intended staying out until this hour, she would have telephoned — she always had telephoned. She hadn't telephoned because she couldn't, and if she couldn't telephone she must be in trouble. The question was, what sort of trouble? She had, as Cordelia very well knew, any amount of enemies — dangerous enemies — and if she'd fallen foul of any of these —

The maid screwed up her small face in an effort of concentration. What could she do? What ought she to do? If only she knew someone who could advise her — Mr. Limpet! The name sprang up before her as though it had literally been written in letters of fire. He would be able to help her. He was so sensible. And he had given her his address in case she might ever want to get in touch with him. She almost ran into her bedroom and fumbled in her bag. Yes, here it was: 'St. Mark's Mansions, Ryder Street, W.1.' A posh address, but, of course, he was only employed there. He was servant to a gentleman, he had told her that much about himself. It was a bit late to go worrying him, nearly eleven, perhaps he'd be cross. She hesitated, torn between her reluctance to risk Mr. Limpet's wrath and her alarm for her mistress' safety. At least she could ring him up and find out whether he could see her. If he could, she could be at Ryder Street in ten minutes by taxi.

His slow, rather ponderous voice

reached her, inquiring the identity of the caller.

'This — this is Cordelia, Mr. Limpet,' she stammered hurriedly. 'Oh, Mr. Limpet, could I see you for a minute? I'm so worried, and I don't know what to do. No, I can't explain over the telephone, but if I could come round for a minute, I can be there in a couple of shakes. Oh, it is kind of you, reely it is!

She slammed the telephone back on its rack and scrambled into her coat, jamming a hat recklessly on her head.

A few seconds later she was in the street looking eagerly for a taxi.

22

Jimmy is Worried

Mr. Limpet turned away from the telephone, rubbing his smooth chin thoughtfully, and wondering whether he had been wise. What possible reason could the girl have for wishing to see him at such an hour? There was no doubt that she was worried — he could tell that by her voice — but what was she worried about? Had he been mistaken in his opinion of her, and was she trying to work some trick? Mr. Limpet shook his benevolent head and looked exactly like a bishop refusing to believe in the sins of the world. Such a thing was impossible. She was genuinely in trouble of some kind and had very naturally turned to him for advice.

A key clicked in the lock as he reached this conclusion, and Jimmy Holland came in. He was followed by the huge figure and smiling red face of Freddie Babbington. Mr. Limpet was a little perturbed. He had not expected his master for another hour, at least, and Cordelia Smith must be already on her way. His face, however, showed only its usual benign expression as he came forward to take their coats and hats.

'I'm earlier than I thought I should be,' said Jimmy. 'Bring the whiskey into the study. Mr. Babbington is going to have one drink, and then I'm going to chuck him out.'

'Excuse me, sir,' Limpet bowed, 'I trust you will not be annoyed, but a friend of mine rang up a short while ago asking permission to see me for a few minutes. I agreed. I hope that will be in order, sir?'

'Of course, Limpet!' said Jimmy.

'But it's a young lady, sir.'

'Good lord!' exclaimed his astonished master.

'Good for you, Limpet!' cried the Hon. Freddie delightedly.

There came a timid knock on the front door.

'There she is,' said the irrepressible

Freddie. 'Don't keep her waiting — and give her my love!'

He suffered himself to be dragged into the study as Limpet went to open the door.

Babbington sighed.

'I'm not appreciated,' he said sadly. 'What about this drink, James? If I'm only to have one, it 'ud better be a big one.'

'It'll be a normal one,' declared Jimmy. 'You're bad enough sober; what you'd be like tight, I should hate to imagine.'

Freddie took the glass he held out, eyed its contents disparagingly, and with a 'Cheerio!' swallowed it at a gulp.

'And now,' he said, 'since you're so infernally hospitable, old boy, I'll go.'

'I'm sorry, but I really am dog tired,' said his friend. 'I've been hard at it for the last week.'

'Don't apologise,' said Babbington. 'Dash it all, old boy, if you can't chuck a fellow out of your own flat, what's the British Empire coming to?' He chuckled and moved out into the hall.

'We'll fix an evening together as soon as I get more time,' said Jimmy, following him. 'Probably — Great Scott!'

He broke off and stared in amazement at the girl whom Limpet was escorting to the door.

Cordelia Smith saw him at the same instant and stopped dead. Her worried little face changed to astonishment, and then to anger.

'So that's the game, is it?' she cried shrilly. 'You set this feller to spy on me, did you, hopin' he'd worm himself into me confidence and get to know things about Miss Kesson — ?'

'Really, Miss Delia, you mustn't speak to Mr. Holland like that — ' The horrified Mr. Limpet was, for once in his life, disconcerted.

'Mr. 'Olland! Mr. 'Olland!' Cordelia's eyes blazed with fury. 'Detective-bloomin'-Inspector 'Olland, you mean! I know the perisher! Blimey! 'E's bin 'angin' round Miss Kesson long enough, pryin' and pokin' his long nose where it ain't wanted — !'

'Please, Miss Delia — ' protested Mr. Limpet faintly.

'An' don't you go Miss Deliain' me!' she flashed furiously. 'I thought you was a

189

gentleman, not a copper's nark — '

'What is all this about?' demanded Jimmy sternly. 'You're Miss Kesson's maid, aren't you?'

'You know very well who I am!' snapped Cordelia. 'A nice dirty trick to play on a girl — I don't think! Sendin' your blinkin' servant to scrape up an acquaintance! Just the sort of lousy trick the p'lice would get up to! 'Ere, let me get out of this place into some clean air!'

Limpet pulled himself together and cleared his throat. Slowly and carefully he explained how he had become acquainted with Cordelia; and as he concluded, light dawned on Jimmy's darkness.

'And she imagines that it was all arranged,' he said, 'by me?'

'Of course it was!' snuffled Cordelia.

'I give you my word it was nothing of the kind,' declared Jimmy. 'I'd no idea you knew Limpet until tonight.'

'That's quite true, Miss Delia,' confirmed Mr. Limpet earnestly.

The girl looked at them doubtfully through her tears. Her ingrained distrust of the police made it very hard for her to accept their word.

She smiled a watery, uncertain smile. 'I — I must look an awful sight,' she said unexpectedly, and groped for a handkerchief. 'But wot with being worried about Miss Kesson — '

'What's the matter with Miss Kesson? Why are you worried about her?' asked Jimmy, suddenly anxious.

She hesitated. To her he was an enemy.

'I think you should tell Mr. Holland, Miss Delia,' said Limpet gently.

'Well — ' Again she hesitated, made up her mind, and plunged into her story. 'It's like this, you see — '

She poured out the whole of her worry in a flood of words that streamed over one another like water over a waterfall.

'She's always let me know,' she concluded breathlessly — 'always. An' I'm sure somethin's happened to 'er.'

Jimmy wasn't at all convinced. He thought that the Angel was very probably staying away for reasons of her own, and there were many explanations for her not having rung up. He did not say what he thought, however, being a tactful man.

191

'If she went to the Holborn Restaurant,' he remarked, 'we can easily find out what time she left.' He looked at his watch and pursed his lips. 'It's a bit late, but I'll see what I can do.'

He went into his study, and they heard him at the telephone. After a long time he returned, and his face was grave.

'I think you have good reason for your fears, Miss Smith,' he said. 'Miss Kesson left the restaurant this afternoon in the company of Mr. Abel Scarthright and three other men. She had to be helped out of the place, and the general opinion seems to be that she was drunk.'

'Oh!' exclaimed Cordelia indignantly. 'She never took enough to — '

'I don't believe she was drunk for a moment!' broke in Jimmy, and his voice was hard. 'I happen to know something about the men she was with. You look after Miss Smith, Limpet. I'm going to find Abel Scarthright.'

'And I'll jolly well come with you, old boy!' said Freddie Babbington determinedly.

23

Mr. Scarthright Tells the 'Truth'

Although he was a confirmed bachelor, Mr. Abel Scarthright lived in a pretentious house on Kingston Hill. The study in which Mr. Scarthright was pacing thoughtfully up and down was a room of comfort — a place of low bookcases and many books, with ancient Persian rugs to blend with the colours of the bindings, and bronzes to tone with the polished floor.

The chairs were massive and inviting, and the big writing-table impressive. But to these pleasant surroundings Mr. Scarthright was giving no attention. With his brow furrowed and his hands clasped tightly behind him, he walked mechanically back and forth, wrestling with the problem which the Angel's disappearance from the house at Horsham had set him. His astonishment when, under cover of darkness, he had returned to the derelict building to put the final stage of his plan into execution and found her gone, had been the greatest he had ever experienced in his life.

He stopped in his perambulation of the room and poured out a drink. It was really useless, trying to conjecture. The only sensible thing to do was to wait and see. He swallowed the neat whiskey and glanced at the clock. Half-past twelve. He would have one more drink and then go to bed.

The neck of the decanter was tilted over the glass when he heard the knocking, and paused, frowning. Who could it be at that hour? Perhaps one of the others. If so, it must be something urgent — something that couldn't be telephoned. The knocking came again, imperious, peremptory. He put back the stopper and set the decanter down. The servants were all in bed, and he would have to let the visitor in himself. He went to the door and made his way to the hall, switching on the lights as he passed. The front door was chained and bolted, and he had some difficulty in dealing with the fastenings. At last, however, it was open, and in the light that streamed out over the steps he saw two men.

'Mr. Abel Scarthright live here?' inquired a pleasant voice, and Scarthright nodded.

'I am Abel Scarthright,' he said. 'Who are you, and what do you want with me at this time of night?'

'I'm Detective-Inspector Holland, of Scotland Yard,' was the reply, 'and I should like a word with you.'

Mr. Scarthright's heart gave a sudden, unpleasant leap. So that infernal woman had gone to the police. Well, he would have to bluff it out.

'It's very late, inspector,' he said. 'I was just going to bed — '

'I'm sorry, but the matter is urgent,' broke in Jimmy curtly.

'In that case,' replied Scarthright, 'you'd better come in.'

He stood aside, and Jimmy and Babbington entered the hall.

'We'll go up to my study,' said Scarthright, closing the door. 'Though I can't imagine what you wish to see me about — unless,' he added, 'it's in connection with the burglary that happened here some time ago?'

'It's nothing to do with that,' answered Jimmy, as they ascended the stairs. 'It concerns Miss Angela Kesson.'

Mr. Scarthright ushered them into the room before he replied, and the interval gave him a moment to collect his thoughts.

'Miss Angela Kesson?' he repeated, in surprise. 'I'm afraid I know nothing about her.'

'I understood that she was a friend of yours,' said Jimmy, watching the man narrowly.

Scarthright shrugged his shoulders.

'I know her, of course,' he announced. 'May I inquire the object of these questions, inspector? If Miss Kesson is in any sort of trouble, I'm afraid that I cannot help you.'

'What sort of trouble do you imagine she's likely to be in?' asked Jimmy.

Again Scarthright shrugged his shoulders.

'I was wondering whether — ' He

hesitated. 'Well you know there have been rumours — '

'Rumours? What sort of rumours?' said Jimmy, as he stopped.

'I don't think you need me to tell you that,' retorted Scarthright. 'If this woman is in any trouble with the police, I'm sure it's what was only to be expected.'

'Miss Kesson is in no trouble with the police,' replied Jimmy.

'Then,' said Scarthright easily, 'I cannot understand the reason for your questions, inspector.'

He returned Jimmy's gaze steadily.

'I tell you,' said the young inspector quietly, 'I am anxious to know Miss Kesson's whereabouts, and since she was last seen in your company, I have come to you.'

Scarthright was a little disconcerted. He had not expected this. So the girl hadn't gone to the police, after all. They apparently had no more idea where she was than he had. The situation required careful handling.

'Do you mean that she is missing?' he said.

'She has not returned home or been seen since she left the Holborn Restaurant with you this afternoon,' replied Jimmy.

The man pursed his thin lips.

'It was a most unfortunate incident,' he said at last, apparently reluctantly, 'and, naturally, I don't like talking about it. That will explain my hesitancy when you mentioned Miss Kesson's name. The fact of the matter is, there was a little trouble yesterday afternoon. My friends and I were lunching in a private room in order to discuss business matters, when Miss Kesson forced her way in. We were naturally a little annoyed, but we couldn't very well be rude, since, of course, Miss Kesson was not a stranger to any of us. We offered her refreshment, and I regret to say that — well, to put it bluntly, she took more brandy than was good for her. We were very distressed, as you can imagine, but we did our best. We managed to get her out of the restaurant and into my car. I drove her a short distance out into the country, hoping that the air would revive her, which it did.

When I brought her back to London she had quite recovered and was very apologetic. That's the whole truth of the matter.' Mr. Scarthright concluded his story with a great show of frankness.

'And where did she leave you?' asked Jimmy.

'At Hyde Park Corner,' replied Mr. Scarthright; 'and she was perfectly normal, except for a headache — which was hardly to be wondered at,' he added, with a slight smile.

'What time was it when she left you?' said Jimmy.

Mr. Scarthright considered.

'I couldn't be certain,' he answered. 'Roughly, I should say, about a quarter to five.'

'I see.' Jimmy stared hard at him. 'Then why, if this was all that happened, did you tell the head waiter that Miss Kesson was your secretary?'

For the fraction of a second, Scarthright was taken aback.

'Well,' he said, recovering himself. 'I — I didn't want them to recognize her. It was not a very nice situation for a girl of

Miss Kesson's class. I said she was my secretary on the spur of the moment.'

Jimmy was nonplussed. The explanation was sufficiently plausible to be true, and although he felt that Scarthright was lying — and lying very cleverly — there was no means of proving it.

'Did Miss Kesson mention where she was going before she left you?' he asked.

'No,' said Scarthright, shaking his head. 'I don't know where she went.'

Jimmy was in the act of opening his mouth to apologise and take his leave when Freddie Babbington, who had been prowling restlessly about the room, suddenly turned and spoke.

'I say, old boy,' he said. 'You're a fearful old liar, aren't you?'

Mr. Scarthright, to whom the question was addressed, stiffened.

'I beg your pardon?' he said coldly.

'A fearful old liar,' repeated the Hon. Freddie cheerfully — 'prevaricator, perverter of the truth, and what-not.'

'What do you mean, Freddie — ' began Jimmy.

'It's here you want it,' said Mr.

Babbington, tapping his forehead complacently. 'You don't mean to say you were taken in by all that guff? My dear old boy. I'm surprised at you! Hasn't it seeped into your intelligence, the one weak spot in this fairy tale we've been listening to?'

'Really, sir — ' said Scarthright angrily; but the Hon. Freddie stopped him with a gesture.

'Not your turn, old boy,' he said pleasantly. 'You just listen for a bit. This lady is supposed to have gate-crashed your jolly old meeting and got tight — helplessly, speechlessly tight — that's what you say? I say it's a lot of drivelling nonsense. She must have mopped up brandy at a hell of a rate to do it, and she wouldn't. Think it over and see how silly it is. She might have got a little woozy, but she wouldn't have got in the condition they say she was in at the restaurant.'

'I assure you — ' began Scarthright.

'You can go on assuring me until you come out in purple spots,' declared Mr. Babbington, 'and even then I shan't believe you. I've met Miss Kesson, and so've you, Jimmy, and I tell you the whole thing's bunkum, bilge, and blithering!'

Quite suddenly Jimmy Holland saw how right he was. It was absurd to dream that the Angel would ever have allowed herself to get in such a state.

'If she was tight,' went on Freddie, 'they must have forced the stuff down her throat, that's all.' He tossed something up in the air and caught it deftly. 'What's this key, old boy?' he said. 'The label says Abbey Lodge, Horsham. I found it on your desk. Is this where you took Miss Kesson for the joy ride?'

'That's mine!' snarled Scarthright, making an ineffective snatch at it.

'Thought it might be,' said Babbington. 'Take a look at it, Jimmy, old boy; it's got fresh lipstick on the label!'

24

The Bluff

The Angel lay on a rather lumpy settee and stared up at the low, cream-coloured ceiling that was just visible in the faint grey light of the approaching dawn that was creeping timorously through the curtained windows.

The gag about her mouth was uncomfortable, and her bound limbs ached. Since the departure of the unknown she had slept a little, thought a lot and experienced an increasing desire for food and drink. It was the latter which really troubled her most. The quantity of brandy which she had been forced to swallow had engendered a raging thirst which became hourly more acute. Was this, she wondered, what he had meant by the painful alternative? Was it his intention to starve her into submission?

She twisted over on her left side with

difficulty and felt a little easier. He had vouchsafed no other explanation, but after tying her ankles and wrists expertly and rendering her incapable of calling for help, had taken his departure, leaving her, to use his own words, 'to decide whether she was going to be amiable or not'. She guessed that he would be coming back during the early hours of the morning to find out — and the morning was fast approaching.

She rolled on to her back again, found that in this position she was, for the moment, a little more comfortable, and remained. He would be coming back soon now, and when he found that she persisted in her refusal to write a letter to the bank he would try the 'alternative' with which he had threatened her.

She could still write the letter as a means to gain time, but she would have to word it in such a way that Mr. Thorpe would only conclude that she had made a mistake. It would save the situation for the moment and in the meanwhile anything might happen.

She heard the dinghy bump softly

against the side of the houseboat half an hour later, and presently the key rasped in the lock, and her captor came in. He was still wearing the mask, and she looked eagerly to see if he had brought her food. He seemed to guess what was in her mind, for he shook his head.

'You shall eat when you have done what I want,' he said. 'I will bring sandwiches back with me. I hope that you have decided not to be obstinate?'

She nodded, and his eyes gleamed.

'That is wise of you,' he said. 'I should have been loath to have had to use persuasive methods, although I had come prepared. You will write the letter?'

Again she nodded, and he came over to her, untied her hands, and with a key unlocked the handcuffs.

'There is paper and pen here.' He pulled open a drawer in the table and took a writing pad, envelopes, and a fountain pen.

She sat up, and he put the pad on her lap. Her hands were so cramped that it was some time before she could write, but he waited patiently.

When at last she had written the note, he read it, nodded approvingly, and placed it in the envelope, which she had addressed.

'It is a few minutes after eight,' he said, as he sealed the flap. 'I should be back by eleven with the photograph.' There was an exultant note in his voice. 'Meanwhile I'm afraid I shall have to tie your hands.' He did so, calmly and methodically, tested the gag and the cords at her ankles, and walked over to the door.

'If you had done this in the beginning,' he remarked, 'you would have saved yourself a lot of unpleasantness.'

A moment later he was gone.

The Angel settled back on the uncomfortable settee. The writing of the letter had gained her a short respite, but it would be a very short one. What would happen when he found out that he had been fooled? That the photograph of Uncle Ebenezer had never been deposited at her bank at all? And suddenly she realised that she had made a mistake. When he found that there was no packet deposited at the bank he would guess that it was still at her flat — that it had always been at her flat, and the knowledge would remove the one safeguard she had had. Knowing where it was he could get it without her assistance. Her heart sank. She had been too clever, and her error of judgment was likely to cost her her life!

25

The Evidence in the Dust

'Well here we are,' said Jimmy Holland a trifle gloomily. 'Though, personally, I'm inclined to think we're chasing wild geese.'

He had stopped the car at the drive gates of Abbey Lodge, and was peering up the dark avenue of gaunt trees as he spoke. After Freddie Babbington's discovery of the key on Abel Scarthright's desk, there had been nothing for it but to follow the lead that it had given; but they had set out without any great hope that it would result in the finding of Angela Kesson. Scarthright had strenuously and angrily denied all knowledge of the girl's whereabouts, and stuck to his original story.

'Well, let's get on with it,' yawned Babbington. 'This is not the pleasantest spot in the world, old boy.'

He went over to the gate, opened it, and together they walked up the weed-grown drive. The dust loomed up before them dark, gloomy and uninviting.

They reached the porch, and Jimmy took the key from his pocket and fumbled for the lock. The door opened easily, and they stepped into the darkness of the hall. The young inspector produced a torch and sent its light flickering about. It showed up the cracked, stained walls and the paper that hung in long, dismal streamers, and the dust that was everywhere.

'Cheerful hole!' grunted Freddie. 'It would be a long time, I should think, before anyone'd want to buy this.'

'Somebody's been here recently, all the same,' said Jimmy, and turned the light on to the floor. 'Look at those footprints.'

Mr. Babbington looked and was duly impressed.

'By Jove, you're right, old boy!' he answered excitedly. 'And I'll bet it was Scarthright! He was right when he said he drove the girl out into the country. This is where he came to.'

'Let's see if we can find any other traces,' said Jimmy, and opened the first of two doors on the right of the square hall. It led into a large room with heavily shuttered windows; but the room was empty and the undisturbed dust on the bare floor showed that nobody had entered it. The other three rooms that opened off the hall proved equally barren.

'Nothing here,' grunted Jimmy, when he had inspected the last of these. 'Let's try the rest of the place.'

There was a door at the side of the big staircase, and opening this, he found himself in a huge kitchen. Here there were more footprints — a double lot, as he quickly noticed.

'Scarthright — if it were he, had a companion,' he said. 'But the companion didn't come in with him by the front door — that's queer.'

'Perhaps the second feller was already here, old boy,' suggested Freddie, and Jimmy agreed that it was possible.

'Hello, what's this?' he exclaimed suddenly, and pointed to a large oblong patch where the dust had been disturbed. 'Looks as though somebody had lain down beside this door — '

'And that's just what it is,' said Babbington. 'That's where they laid Miss Kesson, old boy.'

Jimmy frowned and his mouth set grimly.

'Then she was brought here!' he muttered. 'You were right Freddie. Where does this door lead to?'

He tried the handle, found it was locked, and turned the key that was projecting on the kitchen side.

'A scullery,' he said, flashing his light round, 'and — By the Lord Harry, look here!'

'A woman's high-heeled shoes!' cried Freddie Babbington, peering at the marks in the dust. 'That clinches it, old boy!'

'I think it does,' said Jimmy, 'and it about clinches Scarthright, too! He'll have the devil of a job to explain this away.'

'It's awful, old boy,' he whispered. 'That girl — '

'Well, don't let's talk about it!' snapped Jimmy. 'We'll search the rest of the house, and then we'll get back to London.'

26

The Man Who Appeared

'I'm makin' a perfect nuisance of meself, ain't I?' said Cordelia Smith. 'Comin' round 'ere and keepin' you up all night?'

'Not at all, Miss Delia, not at all,' answered the weary Mr. Limpet valiantly, stifling a yawn. 'It is a pleasure to be of service.'

Cordelia, a rather pathetic little figure, fell asleep in the big armchair, and Mr. Limpet dozed on the opposite side of the fire. It was half-past nine before Jimmy, haggard-faced and weary, came in, followed by Freddie Babbington, and startled them to sudden wakefulness.

'Make some coffee, Limpet,' said Jimmy, flinging his hat down on the settee. 'Boiling hot, and as strong as you like.'

Limpet bowed.

' 'Ave you found out wot's 'appened to

Miss Kesson?' asked Cordelia, blinking anxiously with sleep-blurred eyes.

'No,' replied Jimmy. 'She was taken to a house in Horsham belonging to a man called Phelps, but she's not there now.'

'An 'ouse at Horsham?' echoed the maid, and he nodded.

'Yes,' he said — and told her what he and Freddie had discovered at Abbey Lodge.

He began to pace nervously up and down the room.

'I wonder,' said Cordelia suddenly, 'if that feller 'ad anything to do with it?'

He swung round on her.

'What fellow?' he snapped hastily.

'The chap wot broke into the flat, and wot — ' She stopped abruptly. She had been on the point of mentioning 'Brother Bert', but had realised in time that it was better to keep silent regarding him.

'Tell me about him,' said Jimmy quickly. 'Somebody broke into Miss Kesson's flat?'

'Yes,' answered the maid. 'She said he was after the photograph wot — ' Again she checked herself.

'What photograph?' Jimmy came over

213

and stood looking down at her. Cordelia, a little scared that she had said what she shouldn't have said, stared up at him with a frightened face.

'An old pitcher belonging to Miss Kesson,' she replied. 'Funny lookin' thing — an old feller with whiskers — she calls it 'Uncle Ebenezer' — '

'And you say somebody broke in to steal it?' interrupted Jimmy. 'Why should anybody want to steal an old photograph?'

'I dunno, but that's wot she said,' answered Cordelia. 'She said he must 'ave been after Uncle Ebenezer.'

'It can't have anything to do with her disappearance,' began Freddie, but Jimmy interrupted him. 'We don't know what's got to do with her disappearance,' he said. 'We don't know what Scarthright has up against her; maybe this photograph's something to do with it.' He turned again to Cordelia. 'Where is it?' he asked. 'At the flat?'

She nodded.

'Then we'll go there.' He seized his hat. 'Get your things on, Miss Smith, and take us.'

Jimmy's car carried them to Wyvern Court in under ten minutes, and it was just after ten when Cordelia admitted them to the Angel's flat.

She led the way into the sitting room and went over to the tiny bureau.

'In this drawer 'ere,' she said, stretching out her hand. 'Oh, of course, it's locked. I never — '

'I think I can open it.' Jimmy pushed her aside and took a bunch of keys from his pocket. 'These locks are usually simple enough, and any key of the right size will fit.'

But the lock was not as simple as he had expected. It took him nearly twenty minutes before he succeeded in finding a key on Babbington's bunch that fitted.

'Is this the photograph?' he said, lifting out the picture, which the Angel had brought away from Montgomery Webb's house on the night of the murder.

Cordelia peered over his shoulder.

'Yes, that's it,' she declared, and at that moment there came a knock at the front door.

' 'Scuse me, while I see who it is,' she

said, and hurried from the room.

'What an awful looking thing!' said the Hon. Freddie, as Jimmy stared frowning at 'Uncle Ebenezer'. 'There must be a mistake, old boy, nobody would break in for that. It's shocking! I tell you we're wasting time — '

He broke off as they heard a startled cry from the hall, followed by the sound of a fall.

'Is anything the matter?' called Jimmy, but there was no reply.

'I'll go and see,' said Babbington, and crossed to the door. But he never reached it.

'Don't move, either of you!' snapped a voice, and a man appeared in the open doorway — a man whose face was covered by a handkerchief, and who carried an ugly looking automatic in his right hand.

'Who the devil are you?' demanded Freddie angrily. 'I — '

'Keep still and keep quiet,' snarled the newcomer, 'otherwise I shall shoot. There will be no noise, so no one would hear.'

Jimmy saw the silencer on the end of

the barrel of the weapon and understood.

'What are you doing in this flat?' he demanded. 'Who are you?'

'I've come to collect some property of mine,' answered the unknown. 'I see you have saved me the trouble of looking for it.'

Jimmy glanced at the photograph in his hand.

'Is this what you mean?' he asked.

'Yes,' answered the stranger. 'Put it down on that table, and then get over there.'

'I'll see you in hell first — ' began Jimmy.

'You'll be in hell if you don't!' snarled the other. 'Do as I tell you and be quick.'

Jimmy hesitated, but the pistol moved menacingly, and he decided that discretion was the better part of — suicide. 'There you are,' he said furiously and threw the picture down. The unknown picked it up with one quick movement.

'Now I'll go,' he said, backing towards the door. 'I'm afraid I shall have to lock you in, but — '

A hand came from behind him and

snatched the pistol from his grasp. "'Ere, not so fast, mate!' cried a Cockney voice shrilly. 'You ain't a-goin' just yet. I've got a score to settle with you fer that blinkin' swipe you gave me the other night.' The unknown spun round with a lurid oath to face the overall-clad, grease-covered figure that brandished the pistol. It was 'Brother Bert'!

27

The Hon. Freddie Follows a Trail

'You get over there!' said Mr. Albert Smith truculently, waving the pistol recklessly and advancing into the room. 'I want to know wot all this 'ere's abart.'

'This man took us by surprise — ' began Jimmy. 'If you will — '

'An' who might you be?' demanded 'Brother Bert' suspiciously. 'Wot are you a'doin' in this 'ere flat, that's what I'd like ter know — forcin' your way in an' attacking defenceless gals. Blimey, it's a lucky thing I 'appened to come across!'

'I quite agree with you,' remarked Jimmy. 'I'm Detective-Inspector Holland, of Scotland Yard, and — '

Freddie Babbington chose that moment when his attention was fully engaged to slip quietly out into the hall. An idea had occurred to him, by which he thought he could make himself more useful than by making himself scarce.

He passed a dazed and moaning Cordelia, and let himself out by the open front door. Hurrying down the stairs, he crossed the vestibule, and saw as he emerged into the street a large car drawn up a little way away. The car in which he and Jimmy had arrived was standing immediately opposite the entrance to Wyvern Court; and, leisurely crossing the strip of pavement, Freddie got in, started the engine, and drove off.

He sent the car speeding up the street, turned the corner, swung into another street that ran parallel to the one in which the Angel's flat was situated, and presently came to a stop at the other end, from where he could see the entrance to the flats and anyone who came out. He was fairly confident that he would recognise the man by his clothes, and, lighting a cigarette, he waited.

It was a long wait. He smoked two whole cigarettes and half a third before anything happened. In fact, he was just beginning to think that his cleverness was to be unrewarded, and was contemplating returning to the flat to see what had happened, when a man came quickly out of the entrance, hurried to the waiting car, and was driven off. Freddie lifted his gear-lever and let in his clutch. It was the man who had held them up. There was no mistaking the coat and the hat, although he had, naturally, removed the concealing mask.

Freddie sent the car humming away in the wake of the big saloon tingling with excitement.

* * *

To the Angel, who had no means of telling the time, it seemed an eternity since the unknown had left her. Surely by now he should have returned?

The splash of oars and the creak of rowlocks broke in on her thoughts, and she strained her ears to listen. Was it just a passing boat, or was the unknown returning? The rhythmic sounds came nearer, and presently she heard the nose of the boat bump against the landing stage of the houseboat. He had come back. She braced herself for the ordeal that she felt was at hand. The key turned in the lock, and he came in, closing the door behind him. For the moment he stood looking at her in silence, and then he spoke.

'You have put me to a great deal of trouble, Miss Kesson,' he said, in the familiar muffled, husky whisper. 'But I'm sure you will be pleased to know that in spite of your lying and scheming I have been successful.'

He took an envelope from his pocket, and from it withdrew — the photograph! She stared at it in incredulous surprise, and her face was white. Her one card gone — her last flicker of hope snuffed out. What chance had she now?

The masked unknown read something of what was passing in the Angel's mind from her eyes.

'Yes, the chase is over,' he said, 'and now we come to the kill. I am very sorry to have to destroy anything so beautiful, but I'm afraid there is no help for it.'

He came farther into the small apartment and laid the picture down on the table.

'You have been a great nuisance, Miss Kesson,' he said, 'and it will be a relief to a number of people to know that you can be so no longer. This houseboat in which I spend much of my time during the summer is moored over one of the deepest parts of the river. It is, I believe, nearly sixteen feet to the bottom at this point, and suitably weighted, a person should lie there undisturbed. Luckily the necessary materials for weighting you are within reach — quite a quantity of iron ballast, and several lengths of chain by which it can be attached. I'll get it without further preamble since there is no point in delaying the inevitable.'

He turned and went out, and after a little while she heard him moving about at the other end of the boat. Presently he came back staggering under the weight of an armful of rusty lengths of iron, which he deposited on the door. Once more he departed and she guessed he had gone to get the chains he had mentioned. It would not be long now — a few more minutes at the most, and then —

She took a tight grip of her overstrained

nerves. At least, she would face what awaited her without flinching.

★ ★ ★

Freddie Babbington saw the big saloon come to a stop along the towpath, and the man he was following get out. This latter part of the long journey had been very nerve-racking, for once they were in the country he had had to take infinite precautions to avoid his shadowing being suspected. It had meant keeping well in the rear of his quarry, and risking losing him altogether; but even that was better than that the suspicions of the unknown should be aroused. Twice he had lost the car in front, but his luck had held, and he had picked it up again.

When it turned off the main road towards the towpath he had had to think quickly. He knew the country around Staines well, and he guessed where the car was going. He also knew that if he followed it here he could hardly avoid arousing the suspicions of the man ahead.

He came to the end of the road that

gave on to the towpath, and slowed. Standing up he was able to see over some bushes the saloon come to a stop, and the man get out. The car moved off again, and Freddie came to a decision. He got out of his own machine, and watched to see what the other would do.

He walked a few yards along the bank, and then made his way to the water's edge. Stooping, he fumbled at something, and then stepped down. Freddie guessed a boat, although he could not see, and this put him in a quandary. If the man was going to take to the river it was likely to prove awkward, for he had no boat in which to follow him. It was true he could keep him in sight from the bank, provided he did not shoot over to the other side and disappear down some backwater.

The man was pulling out into mid-stream now, and Babbington was able to get a good view of him — a swarthy-faced individual, with a black moustache. He continued to drive the dinghy towards the middle of the river, making no attempt to turn the prow of the boat either up- or downstream, but keeping to a steady, diagonal course towards the opposite bank.

From the concealment of his clump of bushes the Hon. Freddie continued to watch him, afraid to venture out lest he should be seen and recognised. Presently the man in the boat drew near to a medium-sized houseboat, turned to mark his direction and drew into its landing deck.

Freddie Babbington fetched a long breath.

He went to the edge of the towpath and looked up and down stream. Some distance along there was a boat, but it was quite a good way. However, there was nothing else to do unless he swam across, and that did not exactly appeal to him on a cold day. The houseboat would be in sight all the way, so the unknown could scarcely give him the slip.

He set off, striding briskly along, and evolving a plan of campaign as he went. With the boat he could row over to the other side and drift gently down to the house-boat with the current. His approach would be noiseless, and he would be able to take the man unawares.

He came to the boat at last and discovered that it was a rather large and decrepit dinghy, sadly in need of baling out. Concluding, however, that he was lucky to find a boat at all, he made the best of it. There was only one oar, and he had to stand and use this as a paddle. He got across to the opposite bank, somehow — though he blessed the fact that he hadn't got to negotiate the heavy boat against the current in this fashion — and using the oar over the stern as a rudder, let the boat drift.

It moved quite fast, for the stream was running strongly, and when it got near to the houseboat Freddie set about preventing anything in the nature of a bump. Discarding his makeshift rudder, he leaned over the prow, his hands outstretched ready to catch the edge of the deck before the boat could hit it. He succeeded, and brought the dinghy up against the side without a sound.

Gingerly he got out, tied the boat up to a wooden rail and took stock of his surroundings. The main structure was rather like a railway carriage to which had been added an upper story, consisting of a closed-in deck. There were many windows and a door, the whole painted in dingy white and red. Freddie eyed the windows interestedly. If he could get a peep through one of them he could find out what was taking place within.

He began to tiptoe cautiously across the rotten boarding of the lower deck towards a narrow kind of gangway that ran along on the riverside. There was a queer clanking sound going on inside. and he was curious to know what it was. It sounded as though somebody was doing something with chains on bare boards.

He found a window, and very carefully raised himself from his crouching position until his eyes were just on a level with the side. The glass was so dirty that at first he could see nothing, and then he made out the dim outline of chairs and a settee, and on the settee a girl. He had found the Angel!

She was lying at full length, and there was something about the lower part of her face that puzzled him until it struck him that she was gagged. He was so pleased with himself and excited at his discovery that he forgot that the man he had followed was also somewhere on board.

The first reminder he had of this was a startled oath and a rush of feet and then, as he turned to defend himself, a heavy blow caught him on the side of the head.

He staggered back dazed, and half unconscious, against the railing. Next instant, with a crack of splintering wood, it gave way, and he hurtled backwards into the swirling water of the river.

28

Jimmy Adds Two and Two

' 'E 'it me a whack before I knew where I was,' said Cordelia, rubbing her aching head. 'I jest opened the door, and plonk! That's all I knew about it.'

'The perisher,' grunted 'Brother Bert', scowling. 'An' to think I 'ad him good and proper until you came in and jiggered things up.'

' 'Ow was I ter know?' Cordelia sniffed tearfully.

'It wasn't your fault, Miss Smith,' put in Jimmy tactfully. 'It's a thousand pities we lost him, though.'

The three were in the Angel's sitting room, and none of them, as may be gathered, in a very pleasant frame of mind.

The man in the mask had taken advantage of the distraction caused by the unthinking entrance of Cordelia to launch himself on 'Brother Bert', wrench the pistol from his hand, and make good his escape, locking them in. By the time Jimmy had succeeded in breaking open the door and reaching the street he had disappeared. So, also, the young inspector noticed, had his car and Freddie Babbington. This fact toned down to a certain extent his disappointment. If Freddie was on the track of the man there was still a chance of finding him.

'May I use the telephone?' said Jimmy.

'Use wot yer like,' answered Cordelia graciously, and signed to 'Brother Bert' to make himself scarce. He took his departure as Jimmy lifted the receiver, and gave the number of Scotland Yard. In a few seconds he was talking to Sergeant Scorby.

'Notify all stations and patrols to keep a lookout for my car,' he said, when he had explained the situation. 'I don't want it stopped, but I want to be able to trace it. You understand? Ring me back here' — he gave the Angel's number — 'directly you have any news.'

He hung up. That was all he could do at the moment. If Freddie was following the unknown his route would be seen and noted, for Jimmy's car was well-known. He settled himself down to wait, occupying his mind in puzzling over the photograph. It seemed ridiculous that anyone should go to such trouble and risk to secure such an object, but it was obviously valuable to the unknown.

It was midday when the call came through. Jimmy's car had been found empty and unattended up a side turning leading down to the river at Staines and five minutes after he got the message Jimmy was on his way. A police car picked him up at Wyvern Court, and, immune from traffic regulations, made short work of the distance.

In less than an hour and a half from the time the notification had been received Jimmy was standing beside his abandoned car speculating as to the whereabouts of Freddie Babbington. There was no sign of that large individual or any indication where he had gone to.

'He must have gone a pretty good distance, sir,' said Sergeant Scorby. 'The car's been here nearly two hours.'

Jimmy nodded, his brow furrowed in thought. What had happened to Freddie? He was trying to construct a workable theory as to what had taken place when the local policeman, who had found the car and reported the fact, made a remark that brought him out of his reverie with a jerk.

'Somebody's taken old Bilter's boat over to the houseboat,' said the man, nodding across the water. 'That'll be them boys, I expect. Young varmints, they're allus up to some mischief or other. The other day — '

Before he could recount what happened the other day Jimmy interrupted him.

'Do you mean that dinghy?' he snapped.

The constable nodded.

'Yes, sir,' he said. 'It should be moored alongside the bank. Belongs to old Bilter — '

'Never mind old Bilter,' broke in Jimmy. 'I want to get over to that old houseboat. How can I do it?'

The policeman scratched his head and looked vague. The problem was evidently beyond him.

'Isn't there a boat we can borrow?' said

Jimmy impatiently.

'There's Mr. Rancy's punt,' replied the constable slowly. 'But that's a good way from 'ere. 'Bout a quarter of a mile — '

'That'll do,' said Jimmy. 'Show us where it is.'

'Along the path this way, sir,' said the man of law. 'Yer see where that there white post is?' He pointed.

He swung off in the direction of the white post followed by Sergeant Scorby.

Jimmy strode rapidly towards the punt and reached it a good twenty yards ahead of his panting companion. There was a paddle lying in the bottom, and by the time the breathless Scorby arrived Jimmy had scrambled into the punt and was disentangling the mooring chain.

'Come on, jump in!' he said, and the sergeant obeyed.

'What do you expect to find at the houseboat, sir?' he ventured as Jimmy sent the punt out into midstream.

'I don't know,' came the answer. 'But I'm hoping to find Miss Kesson and Mr. Babbington — and I'm hoping they'll be alive!'

29

Just in Time!

The icy shock of the water counteracted the effect of the sudden blow, and the Hon. Freddie came to the surface spluttering and spitting out pints of foul-tasting river. He made a grab for the edge of the houseboat, and his collar was seized. He caught a momentary glimpse of his recent assailant, and then something struck him heavily on the head, and he passed out in real earnest.

When he came to himself he was lying helpless on the floor inside the houseboat itself, and the first thing his roving eyes saw was the Angel, still on the settee as he had glimpsed her through the dirty window. She was looking directly at him, and he saw recognition in her eyes. He tried to open his mouth, and discovered that he had been gagged, too.

'You've come round, have you?' said

the voice of the unknown. 'Well, that's a pity. It would have been easier for you if you'd remained unconscious.'

Freddie twisted his head in the direction of the voice and discovered that the man was bending over an assortment of rusty iron that littered the floor near the door.

'I suppose,' he continued unemotionally, 'that you followed me from Wyvern Court. I ought to have expected that. It was careless of me. However, it doesn't very much matter since I found out before you could do any real damage.'

He began to pass a length of chain through his fingers as if he were measuring it.

'You certainly won't do any more damage,' he went on. 'You and this very inquisitive lady here will keep each other company on the bottom of the river. I understand drowning is quite a pleasant way of dying.'

Freddie went cold. He understood now what the chain and the rusty iron were for.

'But for your sudden and unexpected

arrival,' said the other, 'everything would have been over by now, and I should have been on my way back to London.'

The Hon. Freddie would have given a lot to put into words some of the things that were passing through his mind, but he could only utter an unintelligible grunt. He cursed himself for a blind, blundering fool. A little more caution and he could have rescued the girl and probably captured this unpleasant piece of work with the scrap-iron as well. As it was, he had thrown away his chance. He looked back at the Angel. She was still watching him, and he was surprised to see no trace of fear in her eyes. By James, she'd got pluck as well as looks!

'I think I'll attend to you first,' said the unknown. He dragged three or four of the rusty iron weights over to his captive's side, threaded the chain through eyelets, and began to wind it round Freddie's body. He took a lot of care over this, making sure that it would not slip. When he had finished he sat back on his haunches and surveyed his handiwork with satisfaction.

'Ladies next,' he remarked pleasantly. 'I'm afraid I shall have to remove you from that settee.'

He stooped over the girl and lifted her, laying her down beside Freddie. Fetching more weights and chains, he repeated his previous procedure.

'And that's that,' he said. 'All that remains now is to drag you out and drop you overboard with dear Uncle Ebenezer's photograph to amuse you.'

He picked up the picture and stuffed it into Freddie's breast pocket.

'There we are,' he remarked, stepping back. 'I'll just make sure there's nobody watching on the towpath, and then — !'

He went out. Freddie would have liked to have said some word to the girl who lay near him but that was impossible. He tried to smile, and she evidently understood, for her eyes responded. It was hell to think of her life being cut short in this way. To drown and slowly rot in the slimy mud of the river's bed.

He heard a shout and a wave of hope broke over him. Was there a chance — after all? The Angel's eyes lighted as the shout was repeated.

Something bumped heavily into the houseboat, and Freddie heard a well-known voice cry:

'I want you!'

There came a shot, and then another, and another. The houseboat rocked under a stampede of feet. There was a crashing of branches, and Jimmy's voice again:

'After him Scorby! The beggar's lamed me!'

And then the door was flung open, and Jimmy, limping badly, came stumbling into the little saloon . . .

* * *

The Angel, fresh and dainty, and presenting no trace of her recent ordeal, put a match to the cigarette between her lips and lay back in her chair.

'I feel,' she remarked, blowing out a thin stream of smoke, 'exactly like the heroine in every thriller I've ever read.'

'And so you ought!' said Jimmy Holland severely. 'A nice lot of worry you've caused us!'

'Have I?' She smiled across the table at him. 'I'm very sorry! How did you manage to turn up so opportunely?'

Jimmy told her.

'Well, you were only just in time,' she murmured; 'in fact, you'd have been too late if your friend, Mr. Babbington, hadn't delayed matters.'

They were seated in the lounge of the Royal Hotel at Staines, where they had taken the starving girl and given her food.

'It's a pity the chappie got away,' said Freddie gloomily. 'Who was he, Miss Kesson?'

She shook her head.

'I've no idea,' she replied. 'I'd rather like to know that myself.'

'But surely,' protested Jimmy in astonishment, 'you must have some idea of his identity?'

'I haven't,' she declared frankly. 'The only thing I know about him is that he was desperately anxious to obtain the photograph.'

'Good old Ebenezer!' said Freddie. 'We've got him, anyway.'

He patted his breast pocket with a grin.

'But you know why he wanted the

photograph?' said Jimmy, and again she shook her head.

'No, I don't,' she answered. 'It's puzzled me a lot, and I'm still curious.'

'I don't understand.' Jimmy scratched his chin in bewilderment. 'Isn't this the reason that Scarthright — ?'

'It has nothing to do with Abel Scarthright at all,' broke in the Angel, 'nor any of his friends.'

'But it was Scarthright who took you to that place at Horsham,' said Jimmy. 'We know that — '

'Oh, yes,' she said, 'but it was my unknown admirer who rescued me from them. I don't suppose anyone was more surprised than Mr. Scarthright when he found I'd gone.'

'I'd like to hear more about this,' said Jimmy firmly. 'Why did Scarthright — '

She stopped him with a gesture.

'I owe you a lot,' she said, 'and I don't want to appear ungrateful but I am not answering any questions, Mr. Holland.'

'But this is a serious matter,' he protested. 'You must — '

'I know just how serious it is,' she

retorted — 'nobody better I assure you. But it's entirely my business, and I'm not talking about it.'

'I think you're being very foolish,' said Jimmy. 'I don't know what you've got against Scarthright and his friends, or what they have against you, but you can't fight these men single-handed — it's ridiculous!'

'I have good reasons,' she said, 'at least, they seem good to me.'

'Well,' he replied, 'I suppose it's your business. After all you're taking the risks; but I should have liked to have helped — not,' he added hastily, 'in my capacity of a detective, but as a friend — if you will allow me to call myself that.'

'You've earned the right — both of you,' she said. 'I shall never forget that I owe my life to you.'

'Oh, that's nothing!' muttered the embarrassed Freddie. 'I wish we'd caught that blighter, though.'

'He shouldn't be difficult to trace,' said Jimmy. 'If the houseboat is his own property, we ought to be able to find him that way. His anxiety to get hold of that photograph is what's puzzling me.'

'And he only wanted it to destroy it, old boy,' put in Freddie — 'don't forget that. He was going to send the beastly thing down with me to feed the fishes.'

'Let's have a look at it,' said Jimmy, stretching out his hand. 'Perhaps we can discover its secret between us.'

Freddie produced it from his pocket and handed it to Jimmy. He drew up his chair, cleared the glass-topped table of its ashtray and matches and, laying the photograph in front of him, studied it closely. But, so far as he could see, there was nothing to account for the unknown wishing it destroyed. The same kind of picture could be found in any family album — there was nothing queer about it at all.

'It's a mystery,' he declared after a long and close inspection. 'There's simply nothing extraordinary about this photograph.'

'Do you think the feller's mad?' suggested Babbington. 'Perhaps he's got a mania for destroying Victorian photographs — anti-whiskers, anti-aspidistras, anti-period sort of thing, eh?'

'Why concentrate on this particular

picture?' said Jimmy, taking his suggestion seriously. 'No, I think we can dismiss that idea. I wish you would tell us where you got this, Miss Kesson.'

'I can't,' she replied. 'I found it, that's all I can tell you.'

'And this man has made several attempts to get it,' muttered Jimmy, his brows drawn together. 'Which argues a desperate necessity for destroying it. That leads to the natural supposition that its existence is dangerous to him.'

'But how?' demanded Freddie Babbington.

'I'm hanged if I know!' declared Jimmy candidly. 'But what other explanation is there?'

'Well, anyway,' remarked Freddie cheerfully, 'we've got the jolly old thing as a souvenir.'

'Yes,' agreed Jimmy seriously, 'and I think I'd like to keep it. It seems to me a dangerous possession, and I should feel happier if the danger was mine and not yours, Miss Kesson.'

'Keep it by all means!' she replied, with a smile. 'The only condition I make is that if you discover its secret you will let me know.'

'I'll promise you that!' said Jimmy, and put 'Uncle Ebenezer' in his pocket. When the secret of the photograph was revealed, it was destined that the Angel should be present, and the revelation was to cause her to faint for the first and last time in her life.

★　★　★

Three days had passed since Jimmy Holland's opportune arrival at the house-boat at Staines had averted a double tragedy, and during the intervening period he had made every effort to discover the identity of the unknown, but without result. Inquiries concerning the ownership of the houseboat led to a dead end. It had originally belonged to a Mr. Flaxman, who had apparently sold it to someone else. Since Mr. Flaxman was dead, it was impossible to discover any details of the transaction. Several people living in the neighbourhood were able to state that they had seen an elderly man in occupation during the previous summer, but their descriptions of him were so vague and so varied that they were useless.

Jimmy got into touch with the Thames Conservancy, for every houseboat-owner has to pay a mooring fee to that august body; but, although the fees had been regularly paid, the name of the owner had not been altered, and it was still registered in the name of Flaxman. He visited the Angel several times, and was welcomed by a smiling and affable Cordelia, a startling contrast to his reception on his earlier visits. And there was a noticeable difference in Angela's demeanour. He was worried for the Angel's safety, irritable at his lack of progress in the other matters, and weary with arguments to try to pacify his dissatisfied superiors, when the news came through that was destined to be the prelude to the end.

It was that undersized and insignificant specimen of humanity, Mr. Syd Higgins, who unconsciously started the ball rolling towards that startling and — to some — dreadful conclusion which was to fill the newspapers for days and cover Jimmy Holland with a cloak of glory.

30

Exit Mr. Higgins

Mr. Syd Higgins had received his further fifty pounds, and in the nature of his kind had spent it and its forerunner in a glorious 'bust' that had left him shaky and penniless. He was sitting in his dingy little room, considering the necessity of replenishing the exchequer by the exercise of his nefarious calling, when it occurred to him that there was an even easier way to obtain the money he so urgently needed. He had read of Mr. Leeming's fate in his favourite evening newspaper, and put two and two together. It is true that he failed to make the correct total, but he arrived at a sum that satisfied him. He concluded that for some reason or other, Mr. Leeming had been 'framed' by the man who had come to him, and he decided that here was his chance for easy money. The source that had supplied the first should supply some more. Although Daniel Phelps was not aware that he knew his identity, he did, for on the last occasion when that gentleman had visited him, Mr. Higgins had taken the precaution of following him home with some vague idea that the knowledge might be useful in the future. And now the bread he had metaphorically cast on the waters was to be returned to him with, he hoped, butter and jam.

He would go to Phelps and suggest that unless he paid a further hundred he, Syd Higgins, might prove a useful witness in Mr. Leeming's defence. If he refused, no doubt Leeming would be prepared to pay.

Mr. Higgins thought it was a good scheme, but unfortunately for him he was not a psychologist and failed to realise the dangerous nature of the man he was contemplating blackmailing. He called at Daniel Phelps, in Queen's Square, at nine o'clock that night, and put up his proposition.

Shortly after midnight a patrolling policeman found the huddled-up body of a man in a telephone-box near Kennington Cross.

He had been stabbed in the back and the doctor stated that he had been dead for just over an hour. As has been said, Mr. Higgins was a bad psychologist.

Jimmy Holland heard of the discovery when he arrived at the Yard on the following morning, but since the case was in the hands of another officer and apparently had no connection with the business on which he was expending all his time and energy, he was only vaguely interested.

It was not until later that he was to realise the importance of Mr. Syd Higgins' murder.

The Angel read in the evening paper an account of the finding of the body, and was very thoughtful, for she instantly recognised the connection between the dead burglar and the group of men who formed her chief interest in life. His had been the name which Mr. Leeming had mentioned in the car on the night when he had attempted the frame-up, and it required no very great stretch of imagination to guess why Syd Higgins had died. For a second or two after she had read the report she contemplated ringing up Jimmy Holland and telling him what she knew, but after a little consideration she dismissed the idea. She would have to disclose more than she wished to, and it might also have the effect of completely ruining her long-cherished ambition. It was better for the time, at any rate, to let things take their course and carry on with the plan, which had suggested itself after her escape from the houseboat.

During the intervening period since then she had been very busy indeed. There had been long talks with old Harker and his son and with 'Brother Bert'. She had visited her lawyer and explained exactly what she wanted done, and he had agreed to expedite the business she had asked him to attend to as quickly as possible. He would have been horrified had he known what lay at the back of the Angel's mind and in what an illegal undertaking he was unconsciously involved. Old Harker listened to her proposals with a grave face and certain misgivings.

'It's a terrible risk you're taking, miss,' he said, shaking his head. 'If anything was to go wrong — '

'It's the only way,' broke in the Angel. 'I've tried every other means, and I've failed.'

'And there's no sayin' you won't fail this time,' retorted the old man. 'An' wot then?'

'Then I shall have to admit myself beaten or try something else,' she answered. 'If you'd rather not be mixed up in it — '

'Whatever you says goes, miss,' interrupted Mr. Harker. 'Both me and Ginger 'ull do anythin' you says. You know that. I was only warnin' you that it's a risk.'

'I know that,' she said. 'But I'm determined to try it.'

'Then we're with you, miss,' declared Mr. Harker. 'You just say what it is you wants done and we'll do it.' The outcome of all this was that on the morning following the death of the insignificant Mr. Higgins, Daniel Phelps received a letter from the estate agents who handled his property stating that the dilapidated house at Horsham had at last been sold. A gentleman by the name of Harker had, through his solicitors, purchased it lock, stock, and barrel, and paid over without demur the highest price the estate agents had felt justified in asking. Mr. Phelps would probably have received this piece of news with more pleasure had he been less worried. As it was, he mechanically signed the deeds, which had accompanied the letter, paid the substantial cheque which arrived later into his bank and promptly forgot the transaction. For the terrors of Cain were weighing heavily on his soul and he bitterly regretted that in a moment of blind panic he had allowed himself to take such drastic steps to silence the blackmailing demands of Mr. Higgins.

In the late evening he could stand the house no longer and decided to go for a walk. The exercise might soothe his ragged nerves. He put on his coat and hat and let himself out into the darkness of the almost deserted square. Turning aimlessly to the right he passed a big closed car with dim headlights standing near the kerb a few doors away from his own house. Cars were common enough in that district and he scarcely noticed it as he walked quickly away. It was a fine night. The sky was scattered with brilliant stars. And then it suddenly became dark.

Daniel Phelps uttered a stifled cry as the heavy cloth enveloped his head, and his hands flew up to grip thin, strong wrists. There was a sickly sweet smell and, even while he struggled, his senses swam. By the time the two men had got him into the waiting car, he was unconscious.

31

Four Helpless Men

There were lights in the empty house at Horsham and figures moved about in the hitherto deserted rooms. Mr. Albert Smith, gloomily smoking a cigarette in the kitchen, looked disparagingly about him and finally let his gaze rest on his sister, who was poking the fire, which had been lighted in the big rusty range.

'Wot I want to know.' he said suddenly, 'is wot's the idea? That's wot I want ter know, see. Wot time did Miss Kesson say she was coming down?'

'Round about ten o'clock,' answered Cordelia. 'She ought ter be 'ere any minute now. I'm just goin' ter make some tea so as it 'ull be ready for 'er when she gets 'ere.'

He raised his head suddenly and listened.

'There's the car now,' he said. 'That'll

be Miss Kesson.'

Cordelia picked up the teapot, which was warming on the hob, and began to measure out tea from a packet.

'Don't stand there doin' nothin', Bert!' she called shrilly. 'Get them cups and saucers and fetch the milk from the scullery.'

Mr. Smith obeyed clumsily, and the maid was pouring the boiling water into the pot when the Angel entered. Her face was flushed with the keen air and her eyes were bright.

'All the guests comfortable?' she inquired gaily.

'As comfortable as they could be, tied up like they are,' said Mr. Harker. 'They ain't 'ad nuthin' to eat since me and Ginger brought 'em 'ere.'

'That won't hurt them,' said the Angel calmly. 'I'll go and see them in a minute. Is that tea you have there, Cordelia?'

'Yes, miss. I've just made it fresh. I thought you'd like a cup after your journey.' She brought a steaming cup over and gave it to her mistress.

The Angel sipped it gratefully.

'That was nice,' she said, putting down the empty cup. 'Now we'll attend to business.'

She left the kitchen and returned to the bare hall. Pausing outside a door on the right she turned the handle and entered the large room beyond. It was dusty and devoid of furniture. The shutters had been closed over the windows and blankets hung to avoid any possibility of the light from an oil lamp, which stood on the mantelpiece, showing outside. Leaning against the wall reading a paper was Ginger, and on the floor, their backs resting against the blank wall, sat four men, securely bound and helpless.

'Good evening, gentlemen,' said the Angel sweetly. 'This is not quite so comfortable as a private room at the Holborn Restaurant, but infinitely less public.'

Four pairs of eyes looked at her with varying expressions.

'So you're responsible for this — this outrage?' croaked Abel Scarthright huskily. 'What do you think you're going to get out of it, eh? What's the idea?'

'That you will learn in due course,'

retorted the Angel. 'Presently I am going to tell you a little story, and then quite a lot of things will become clear.'

'Do you think you can get away with this?' demanded Jonathan Bellman. 'Sending out thugs to bring us here and then keeping us prisoners in — '

'I have got away with it,' replied the Angel calmly. 'You're here in proof of the fact.'

'But we shall be missed,' snarled Daniel Phelps. 'You fool, you don't imagine that you can kidnap four businessmen and not have the police making enquiries — '

'The police can make as many enquiries as they like,' said the girl, 'but they won't help you.'

'Where have you brought us?' said Scarthright. 'What is this beastly place?'

'You ought to know,' answered the Angel. 'You brought me here first.'

'I?' cried Scarthright, and then as her meaning dawned on him: 'Do you mean that this — that this is — '

'It was Mr. Phelps's house,' she said. 'I bought it the day before yesterday.'

'Good heavens!' There was consternation

in Phelps' voice. 'You bought it? But it was a man called Harker — '

'My nominee,' said the Angel.

'Why have you done this?' said Hathaway. 'Why have you brought us here?'

'I want information,' snapped the Angel quickly, and her eyes were hard. 'I've tried other means to get it and now I'm going to try this. I want to know which of you killed Leonard Drake.'

A sharp sound like the sudden release of pent-up steam came from where they were sitting, and the four faces seemed to grow whiter in the dim light.

'You — you're mad!' It was Scarthright who spoke. 'Mad! The man who killed Leonard Drake was tried and found guilty and — hanged.'

'A man was tried, and found guilty and hanged,' said the Angel, and her voice was like chilled steel. 'But he was innocent.'

'Nonsense!' snarled Daniel Phelps. 'Easthanger was as guilty as hell. You're crazy, girl! Anyhow, what's it got to do with you?'

'I'll tell you,' replied the Angel,

'because that is one of the reasons I have had you brought here. Six years ago a man called Leonard Drake was shot dead in the grounds of Lord Easthanger's estate in Hampshire. Lord Easthanger was found by a gardener standing over the body with a revolver in his hand. It was proved that the bullet, which had killed Drake, had been fired from that revolver and that Lord Easthanger had had an appointment with Drake, at the place where the murder was committed, for that evening.

'The gardener had heard the shot a few minutes before he made the discovery, and had seen nobody else in the vicinity except his master. There was every reason why Lord Easthanger should have killed Drake, because Drake had been blackmailing him for years. Lord Easthanger was arrested and, as you said just now, tried, found guilty and hanged. He had a wife and child. The shock of his disgraceful death killed his wife, but the child did not die. She swore to clear her father's name, for she knew, because he told her, that he was innocent. She is here before you now. She was eighteen then, and for six years she has dedicated her life to finding out the truth. You asked the other day who I was. Well, now you know. I am Angela Easthanger, the daughter of the man who was executed for a crime he never committed!'

32

Mr. Leeming Talks

Mr. Oscar Leeming, in the discomfort of his cell, found ample opportunity for thought. His thoughts were by no means pleasant ones, but since he had very little power over them, he could not help that. He summoned the officer in charge of his temporary prison and declared that he wished to make a statement. And when the formalities had been complied with, a statement he made.

It was a long statement, and it contained, without any omissions whatever, a full and true account of the incidents that had led up to and resulted in Mr. Leeming's arrest and present incarceration. The whole plot regarding the frame-up against the Angel was laid bare.

Jimmy Holland was brought into conference, since anything appertaining to the activities of the Angel was his particular province and the immediate result was that a visit was paid to the house of Daniel Phelps by Jimmy and the inspector who was inquiring into the death of Mr. Higgins, armed with a warrant for the arrest of Daniel Phelps on a charge of wilful murder.

Unfortunately, the warrant could not be executed, for Mr. Phelps was not there.

'He's bolted!' grunted Inspector Redman, and at first Jimmy agreed that it looked very like it. At Scarthright's house they were confronted with a similar situation. Abel Scarthright had set out for his office on the previous day and had not returned. Jimmy looked at the puzzled Redman and frowned.

They tried the others, but they did not find them. Hathaway and Bellman had vanished as completely as had Daniel Phelps and Abel Scarthright.

'There can't be any doubt about it now,' declared Inspector Redman, with conviction.

Jimmy was silent. It looked to him very

much as though the Angel had had something to do with these sudden disappearances, but he kept this idea to himself. It was now late in the afternoon, and when he had got rid of Redman, he drove to Wyvern Court and went up to the Angel's flat.

But there was no reply to his ring, and he had turned disappointedly away when he ran into Freddie Babbington.

'Hello, hello!' greeted that large individual cheerfully. 'Have you just arrived or are you just going, old boy?'

'I was just going,' replied Jimmy. 'Apparently there is nobody in.'

As they descended in the lift he briefly told his friend what was worrying him.

'Well, what about going along to your flat for a spot and chew the thing over?' suggested Babbington.

Jimmy thought this was a good idea. They were admitted by the dignified Limpet, and drinks were brought into the little study.

'Maybe this chappie of the houseboat is at the bottom of it,' said Freddie.

This had not occurred to Jimmy.

'I don't see what he would want with Scarthright and the others,' he said. 'He was only after the photograph.'

'There may have been something else as well,' said Freddie. 'We know nothing about that nasty piece of work who tried to cut short my young and valuable life. By the way, you've got Uncle Ebenezer, haven't you?'

'Yes.'

'Trot him out old boy, and let me have a look at him,' said Freddie. 'I've never had a real good worry at him. Perhaps I can wrest the dark and grisly secret from him.'

'You'll be even cleverer than you think you are if you can,' said Jimmy. He unlocked the safe and produced the photograph. 'There you are. It will keep you quiet, anyway, and that's something.'

Freddie Babbington settled himself comfortably in his chair, and stared at the elegant gentleman with his beautiful whiskers, the gilt chair, and the marble pedestal and aspidistra. Jimmy, lighting a cigarette, began to pace up and down the room. He was more worried than he cared to admit, for if the Angel was responsible for the disappearance of these men it might be a serious matter for her. But if, for reasons of her own, Angela had taken the law into her own hands and carried these men off somewhere, she was likely to get into trouble, and Jimmy did not want that to happen. In fact, he would have gone to almost any lengths to prevent it. But perhaps he was imagining things. Even now the girl might be comfortably reading a book in front of her sitting room fire.

He picked up the telephone. That could easily be proved, anyway. He gave her number and waited. After a long delay the voice of the operator informed him that there was no reply.

'No answer, old boy?' asked Freddie, looking round as Jimmy hung up the receiver.

Jimmy shook his head.

'Darned funny!' commented Mr. Babbington. 'That maid of hers ought to be in, anyhow.'

Jimmy made no reply, but took up the telephone directory and rapidly turned the pages. An idea had occurred to him, which was easy to test. He found the number of Harker's garage and tried to get through. But there was no reply from here, either. He was pretty sure now that his idea was right and that the Angel was responsible. She had enlisted the aid of the people in the garage, whom he had every reason to believe to have been in her pay. He made up his mind quite suddenly.

'Come along!' he said. 'I'm going to Wyvern Court.'

'But, my dear old boy,' protested Freddie, 'what's the good, if they're all out?'

'I'm not going to try the front entrance,' said Jimmy. 'I'm going up the fire escape. There's a balcony and french windows, and a penknife will admit us.'

He was out in the hall before he had finished speaking and pulling on his coat. Freddie hesitated for a second, thrust 'Uncle Ebenezer' into his breast pocket, and joined him.

They were at Wyvern Court in ten minutes, and in another ten were standing on the balcony.

'In you go!' he said, in a whisper, and Freddie stepped into the darkness beyond. Jimmy followed him, felt his way to the door and pressed the switch. When the lights came on he glanced about him. The place was very neat, and almost the first thing he saw was a legal-looking document lying on the top of the little desk. He went over and picked it up, and his exclamation brought Freddie Babbington to his side.

'What is it?' he asked.

'The title deeds of Abbey Lodge, Horsham,' said Jimmy. 'Made out to Harker. I was right. The Angel has bought that old house of Phelps's, and I'll bet a pound to a penny that she's taken those four men there!'

33

The Catastrophe

If the Angel had intended to cause a sensation by the revelation of her identity. she was not disappointed. Incredulity, astonishment, and consternation flitted in swift succession across the faces of the four men in from of her.

'Easthanger's daughter!' muttered Abel Scarthright. 'My God!'

'You never guessed?' said the Angel. 'I'm surprised it didn't occur to you.'

'We thought you'd gone abroad with your mother,' whispered Julian Hathaway hoarsely. 'Everybody thought so — '

'And everybody was wrong,' she interrupted. 'We went to Camberley when the estate was sold, and lived in a cottage in the name of Smith. Mother died there, and was buried in the churchyard. There is no name on the stone that marks her grave. When my father's memory has been publicly cleared, her real name will be inscribed there.'

'You're crazy, girl!' exclaimed Jonathan Bellman angrily. 'Your father killed Drake. There's no doubt of it. The evidence against him was irrefutable — '

'I care nothing for the evidence,' said the Angel. 'I went to see my father in prison while he was awaiting execution. I went with my mother; it was the last time we saw him, and he swore then that he was innocent. He would not have lied to us.'

'But why should you think we know anything about it?' said Daniel Phelps. 'What do you expect to get from us?'

'The truth,' she answered quietly. 'You know how Drake died, and who killed him, and you will tell me. That's why I've brought you here.'

Bellman uttered a short laugh.

'You've had your trouble for nothing!' he snarled. 'I've never heard such nonsense! Of course Easthanger killed Drake — '

'I'm afraid you've rather let your imagination get the better of your intelligence,' put in Daniel Phelps smoothly. 'I assure you you've made a very big mistake, and a mistake that is likely to land you in serious trouble. In forcibly bringing us here and keeping us against our wills you have perpetrated an offence in the eyes of the law. We are, however, reasonable men. Now that we know who you are, we understand something of the feelings that have prompted you to act in this way. We not only understand them, but in a great measure we respect them. I give you my word, however, that you are wrong, and that we know nothing about the death of Drake that is not already public property. He was a business associate of ours, but we had no knowledge of the fact that he was blackmailing your father until it came out in evidence at the trial. Now, why not be sensible: admit that you've made a mistake and release us from this unpleasant and intolerable position? I'm sure we shall all be prepared to overlook what you have done and say no more about it.'

'Have you finished?' inquired the Angel, as he paused. 'A most admirable and appealing speech, but really only a waste of breath. I have no intention of releasing any of you until I get the truth.'

'You've had the truth!' snapped Bellman. 'I second everything Phelps has said. Let us go and we won't make any trouble.'

'You won't make any trouble, anyway,' she retorted. 'You've forgotten that very convenient well in the garden into which I think you planned to put me.'

The faces before her paled visibly in the light of the lamp.

'My God!' cried Scarthright. 'You don't intend to murder us?'

'It will depend on you,' said the Angel — and there was inexorable purpose in her eyes.

★ ★ ★

Into the Angel's mind crept a doubt. Had she made a mistake? Were none of these men, whom she had suspected, guilty? Were all her efforts and her risks to come to naught? It was impossible. It must be one of them. Everything she had discovered about them proved how unscrupulous they were. She was allowing herself to be talked over and these men were adepts in the use of smooth speech. Certainly there was the possibility that the murderer was not among them. It might have been Montgomery Webb or Oscar Leeming, but she had based her scheme on the conviction that the killing of Drake had been a conspiracy in which they were all concerned. She steeled herself and crushed down her vague doubts.

'Well,' she said coldly, 'I don't intend to argue the matter further. I've told you what I want, and you will get neither food nor drink until you decide to speak — '

She broke off with a startled cry, for Bellman suddenly sprang to his feet and came charging towards her. It flashed to her brain that during the time they had been talking he had managed somehow to free himself — and then he was clawing at her with strong, murderous fingers. She tried to fight him off, and opened her mouth to call for help; but his hands were at her throat, and the cry was choked before it was born. They staggered across the bare room and brought up against the mantelpiece. Its sharp edge caught the Angel across the back, and she felt herself go sick and dizzy with the pain. There was a crash, and sudden darkness was followed almost instantly by a brighter light that flickered strangely.

Bellman flung her from him, and she nearly fell into the blazing oil, which was streaming from the broken lamp over the wooden floor. Instinctively however, she gripped the mantelpiece and saved herself. She saw, dazedly, old Harker appear in the doorway just as Bellman reached it and grappled with him. They swayed back into the room, and the Angel stumbled towards them, watching for an opportunity to help Harker, but before she could find one, Bellman had forced his adversary to the door, and with a well-planted blow sent him staggering through. The old man crashed into his son, and they both fell heavily.

Bellman was halfway across the threshold when the Angel caught at him and tried to pull him back. He turned on her with a snarl of fury and attempted to break free, but she clung on desperately, calling loudly for help. He changed his tactics so suddenly that she was unprepared. Instead of trying to break away, he dragged her with him into the hall, just as Cordelia and 'Brother Bert' appeared on the scene. The maid uttered a shrill scream and rushed to her mistress' assistance, but Bellman, his face distorted with rage, picked up the Angel and flung her with all his strength at the other girl. They fell together in a confused heap, and Bellman turned to meet 'Brother Bert' as that little man made a rush at him.

Smoke was pouring now in a thick cloud through the open doorway of the dining room, and the vicious crackling of burning wood added to the din and rose above the frantic shouting of the three helpless men. Old Harker got shakily to his feet and went to 'Brother Bert's assistance, but a blow from Bellman which missed the little burglar caught him unluckily full on the chin and sent him sprawling. Bellman, panting and almost spent, hooked his foot behind 'Brother Bert's' ankles, and at the same time planted a short-arm jab in his stomach.

Mr. Smith uttered a gasping groan and

went staggering backwards into the burning room. Bellman gave a hoarse grunt of triumph, pulled the door shut, and turned the key, ignoring the smothered cries of his associates. As the Angel came unsteadily to her feet he pulled the key from the lock and darted for the front door. She went after him, calling to Ginger. But that unfortunate youth had struck his head violently in falling, and was only semi-conscious.

Bellman dragged the door open before she could reach him, slammed it in her face, and, plunging down the steps, went racing towards the drive. As he reached the dark avenue he flung the key, which he held, from him into the shrubbery. His heart was hammering in his chest, and there was a dull pain in his side. If the blood had not been beating in his ears he would have heard the car approaching. But he heard nothing, and the first warning he had of its presence was the two glaring white circles of light that sprang suddenly out of the blackness to meet him as he rounded the bend. He tried to dodge them, but it was too late.

Something caught him and hurled him up in the air. He uttered a thin, breathless scream and fell, to lie motionless on the hard gravel . . .

Jimmy Holland brought the car to a skidding stop and got out, followed by Freddie Babbington. He had seen the running figure too late to avoid it.

'Is he hurt?' asked the Hon. Freddie, nervously and rather foolishly, as Jimmy bent over the still form.

'He's not dead,' answered Jimmy, with relief. 'Though he'd only have himself to blame if he were. Of all the dam'-fool things — running round that bend like that! He must have heard us.' He caught his breath suddenly. 'Good God — it's Bellman!'

'Bellman? That's one of the fellers we're looking for, isn't it, old boy?' said Freddie.

Before Jimmy could reply, the uneven sound of running feet reached them, and they looked round. Into the car's brilliant lights came the figure of a girl, and they recognised the Angel. Her face was white and strained.

'Angela — ' began Jimmy — and she gave an exclamation of thankfulness as she saw who it was.

'Oh, it's you!' she panted. 'Have you caught him — Bellman?'

'I'm afraid we have,' he answered. 'He ran full tilt into my car. I think he's injured — '

'Never mind that,' she interrupted impatiently. 'Has he got the key?'

'The key? What key?'

'The key of the dining room!' She spoke with difficulty. 'The key of the dining room! The others are in there — helpless — and the room's on fire!'

34

Two From Four

For the fractional part of a second Jimmy Holland stared in horror at the strained, white face of the girl before him, and then he acted. Wheeling round he dashed to where the unconscious Bellman lay, and, stooping, began to search his pockets. He found a bunch of keys among other things but no single key. Neither was there anything in the man's hands.

'There's no key here,' he said. 'Probably he dropped it when the car hit him.'

'I'll have a look — ' began Freddie Babbington, but the Angel cut him short.

'There's no time to look!' she cried. 'We must break down the door.' She was flying back towards the house before she had finished speaking.

'You stay here with Bellman,' said Jimmy to Freddie, and followed her. Cordelia Smith met them in the porch sobbing hysterically.

'Bert — Bert's in there!' she wailed. 'Bert an' them others, and they're screaming something horrible. Fer 'Eaven's sake do somethin' or 'e'll be burnt to death!'

Jimmy's face set. The hall was full of smoke, and old Harker was attacking the stout door with a broken chair.

'Let me try.' Jimmy took the chair from the helpless man, but at his first blow it smashed to pieces in his hand.

He flung the remains of it away.

'We're wasting time,' he said. 'What about the windows?'

'The shutters are fastened inside,' said the Angel. 'And — '

'That doesn't matter,' he snapped. 'They'll be easier to smash than the door.'

He ran out into the darkness and round to the windows. The remains of a rockery provided him with a heavy lump of concrete, and with this he smashed the glass. Eddies of smoke curled out from the joints in the shutters beyond, and the acrid smell of burning wood stung his nostrils. A confused jumble of oaths and screams came dully to his ears as he frantically attacked the shutters. Blow after blow he rained on them with the heavy implement before, with a sharp crack, the fastenings gave and the shutters flew inwards. A wave of burning air rushed out together with a billow of thick, choking smoke. He could see a red glare and yellow-white flames came leaping and dancing through the aperture he had made. Jimmy tore his handkerchief from his pocket and bound it hurriedly round his mouth and nose, and pushing the broken shutters wider, clambered into the blazing room.

The heat was terrible. It burned his flesh and made him gasp for breath, and almost blinded him. Through streaming eyes he peered about, hastily made out a dim shape near the door round which the flames were licking, and stumbled over to it. Holding his breath, for even with the handkerchief it was impossible to breathe that scorching air, he stooped, groped for a hold, and succeeded in lifting the limp figure up. With bursting lungs and burning eyes he staggered back to the window and thrust his burden on to the sill. The Angel and Harker were standing outside anxiously and willing hands assisted him. The unconscious 'Brother Bert' was handed out into the cool air and Jimmy, after gulping some of it into his tortured lungs, turned back into the inferno of smoke and flames, guided by the groans and faint cries which rose spasmodically above the roar and crackle of the fire. He stumbled over a limp body, gripped it, and dragged it blindly to the window. It was as much as he could do to hoist it up, for he was nearly spent. But he managed it somehow, though the effort left him gasping and weak.

'Jim, don't risk any more — come out!' The Angel's voice, high-pitched with anxiety, came to him clearly, but he shook his head and once more plunged into the raging furnace that now surrounded him. His eyes were useless. He could only dimly see, and the pain in them was agonizing. His clothes were alight in several places, and his hair was singed.

'Jim, come back. For Heaven's sake come back.' The appeal reached him faintly and, it seemed, from a very long way away. He stumbled and almost fell, recovered himself, and tried desperately to find the men he was trying to save. But in his blindness he was searching in the wrong part of the room. The heat was now appalling. His skin seemed to be shrivelling, and his flesh felt raw. A great tongue of flame leapt up and curled round him, and his senses swam. Burnt, blackened, and choking, he groped unsteadily for the window, reached it, and fell unconscious across the sill . . .

★   ★   ★

Jim Holland opened his smarting eyes to a cool breeze and became aware that his forehead was being gently bathed. Regaining full consciousness he discovered that he was lying with his head pillowed in the Angel's lap. An uncertain reddish light flickered and danced behind her, and the air was strongly aromatic with the smell of burning.

He looked up into the girl's face, and she saw that he had recovered.

'Better?' she asked softly.

'Yes. I'm quite all right.' His voice was cracked and hoarse. 'What happened? Did you get those men out?'

'No.' She shook her head. 'The rest of the ceiling fell just after Harker and I succeeded in dragging you out through the window. In another second you, too, would — '

She finished the sentence with a little shiver. Jimmy sat up stiffly and looked beyond her. The old house was blazing furiously. Great white and orange flames hissed and darted skywards from a glowing red furnace. Billows of smoke rolled sluggishly over the burning building, and showers of sparks shot upwards intermittently as portions of the interior of the doomed structure gave way and fell.

'Can nothing be done?' muttered Jimmy.

'Harker has taken the car and gone to give the alarm,' said the Angel. 'But I think it will be too late.'

She rose to her feet and turned to survey the holocaust.

'Which' — Jimmy scrambled up and came to her side — 'which of those men — '

'You saved Julian Hathaway,' she answered quickly, before he could complete the question, 'and — and a man who is employed by Mr. Harker. Daniel Phelps and Abel Scarthright are — still there.'

'Poor devils,' said Jimmy soberly. 'What a dreadful end.'

There was a crash and a great fountain of flame and sparks gushed upwards.

'Part of the roof's gone,' said Jimmy. 'The whole place'll be gutted. There's not a chance of saving it now.'

He turned towards the drive looking for the lights of his car, but there was no sign of them or it.

'Mr. Babbington took Bellman and Hathaway into Horsham to a doctor,' said the Angel, answering his unspoken question. 'They were both badly injured and he thought they ought to have medical attention at once.'

'Quite right,' agreed Jimmy, and suddenly: 'Listen!'

The first notes of a jangling bell

reached them, growing louder and louder.

'The fire engines,' said Jimmy and a few seconds later they came rushing up the drive, the brass helmets of the men who manned them turned to copper in the ruddy light.

But fifty engines could not have saved the old house then. The fire had gained too big a hold. Dawn began to streak the east, and the firemen were still fighting a losing fight. The sun, pale and without heat, rose shedding its yellow light on a blackened structure of red-hot brick and smouldering wood from which rolled clouds of steam and smoke and around which the figures of the firemen still moved untiringly.

35

The Secret of the Photograph

Jimmy Holland gave a sharp rat-tat with the small chromium-plated knocker on the Angel's front door and waited. After a slight pause it opened and Cordelia appeared on the threshold.

'Oh, it's you!' she said, and her small face broke into a smile. 'Early, ain't yer? Miss Kesson's in her bath, but you can go in.'

'I wouldn't dream of such a thing,' declared Jimmy gravely. 'Let Miss Kesson finish her ablutions in the privacy which is suitable to such occasions. I will wait in the sitting room.'

'That's what I meant, yer know that very well,' said Cordelia indignantly. 'Get along with yer!'

Jimmy grinned, and entered the cosy little lounge.

'Would you like some cawfee?' asked

the maid, lingering at the door

Jimmy shook his head.

'No, thanks!' he said. 'I'll wait until Miss Kesson emerges from the bath.'

Cordelia left him, and lighting a cigarette he strolled over to the window and stared down into the street. It was the morning of the day following the fire at Horsham and he looked drawn and worn out, for he had very little sleep for two nights. In his frantic attempt to rescue Phelps and Scarthright he, too, had suffered several baddish burns, and although these had been dressed, they still pained him. Throughout the day the old house had smouldered; the debris so hot that it was impossible until the evening to search for the bodies of the two men who had perished in the flames. Even then only the firemen in special protective suits could enter the ruins. They discovered the charred remains under a heap of hot embers, bearing very little semblance to anything human and completely beyond recognition. They were removed to the mortuary at Horsham to await the inquest, and this was rather troubling Jimmy, for he did not see how he could avoid dragging the Angel into it. After all, she had taken them to the house and was to a certain extent responsible for what had happened. It was true that Bellman had started the fire in his dash to escape, and but for his locking the door of the burning room they could have been easily saved. All the same, a public inquiry was going to be very unpleasant for the girl. He was still frowning over this when she came in wrapped in a silken dressing gown and bringing with her a delicate aura of bath salts.

'You're an early visitor,' she greeted. 'Have you had breakfast?'

'Two hours ago,' he replied. 'But I'll have a cup of coffee with you if you ask me.'

'Consider yourself asked!' said the Angel gaily, and touched the bell. 'I suppose,' she went on, 'that this is not entirely a friendly call? You want something, don't you?'

'It doesn't sound very complimentary, but you're quite right,' he answered. 'I want the truth.'

'I thought that's what you might have come for,' she said quietly.

He waited, expecting her to go on, but she remained silent. He was just on the point of opening his mouth to tell her how necessary it was that she should confide in him, when Cordelia entered with a laden breakfast tray.

She set it down on a low table near the fire and paused in the doorway just as she was going out.

'I 'spose Bert 'ull 'ave ter go back ter Pentonville?' she said.

'I'm afraid he will — when he comes out of hospital — which won't be for several days,' answered Jimmy, to whom she had addressed the question. 'There's nothing seriously the matter with him, but he's had a bad shock and one of his arms is severely burned. However, I'll do my best for him — '

'It won't do 'im no 'arm to finish his stretch,' said Cordelia. 'But I wanted ter know if — will it 'ave ter come out that I'm 'is sister —' She stopped abruptly, fidgeting nervously, her small face reddening. 'Yer see,' she went on suddenly, 'I wouldn't like — If Mr. Limpet knew that me brother was a crook — '

A light broke on the momentarily astonished Jimmy.

'Don't you worry about that, Cordelia,' he said. 'There's no reason why Limpet should know anything about your brother, but even if he did know, it wouldn't make any difference to you. I know Limpet well enough for that.'

Cordelia, crimson with embarrassment, gasped a mumbled word of thanks and hastily departed.

'Well what do you know about that?' said Jimmy. 'Limpet has apparently made a conquest. There's some advantage in looking like an archbishop after all.'

The Angel handed him a cup of coffee.

'There are also a number of advantages in not,' she remarked. 'Personally, I prefer the more athletic type of man.'

'Like me?' suggested Jimmy, and she coloured.

'I was speaking generally,' she retorted, and hastily changed the subject. 'How is Bellman?'

'Bad,' he replied. 'Concussion and a

fractured leg. It's a toss up whether he pulls through.'

'I can't say I'm very sympathetic,' she said. 'It was a wicked thing to lock that door. He knew the lamp had set the room on fire.'

'I can't imagine why he did it,' said Jimmy. 'It wasn't necessary for his escape.' He paused and then went on: 'Look here. Reverting to the reason for my having inflicted myself on you so early — are you going to tell me all about it?'

She was a long time answering.

'I suppose I may as well,' she said at last. 'It doesn't matter very much now. All my hopes and schemes have come to nothing, anyway.'

She began in a low, hesitant voice to repeat what she had told the four helpless men at Horsham on the night of the tragedy.

Jimmy listened in growing amazement.

'So that's it, is it?' he said, when she finally ceased speaking. 'You really are an amazing girl. Why didn't you take the police into your confidence?'

'What would have been the use?' she

asked. 'They were convinced that daddy was guilty. Everything had been tried to save him. An appeal, everything — they wouldn't have listened to me. I had no proof, nothing but the fact that I knew he was innocent. Harker believed it, too. He was our chauffeur and knew me since I was a little tot. He was ready to do anything to help me, for he was very fond of my father and mother. I had very little to work on, but I found out that Drake was associated with these other men and that their reputations were not of the best. I concluded that as my father had not killed Drake it was more than likely that one of these men had, and I set out to try to prove my idea. I was not successful. It doesn't look now as if I'm ever likely to be,' she added bitterly.

'And how do the photograph and the unknown man who took you to the houseboat come into it?' he asked.

'They don't,' she replied. 'They've got nothing to do with it at all.' She hesitated. 'Since I've told you so much I may as well tell you everything,' she continued. 'I was at Montgomery Webb's house on the night he was murdered. I went there with the intention of searching his papers for the evidence I was seeking. And I found him — dead. His murderer was still there when I arrived, and during his escape he dropped that picture.'

'Then the man who killed Webb is the mysterious individual who has been after the photograph?' said Jimmy.

She nodded.

'Yes,' she said, 'now you know as much as I do.'

He frowned and rubbed his chin.

'What is worrying me,' he said, after a little while, 'is how I'm going to prevent all this coming out. That's why I wanted you to tell me the truth. There'll be an inquest on Scarthright and Phelps and the coroner will want to know how they came to be in that house at all.'

'Does it matter whether it comes out or not?' she asked wearily. 'I don't mind. I've failed and that's all that matters.'

'It's not all that matters,' said Jimmy angrily. 'The only thing that matters is keeping you out of it. Oh Lord, you have got yourself into a mess, haven't you?'

'And I'll have to take the consequences,' said the Angel. 'I've always been prepared for that in case anything went wrong.'

'Did you find out anything about these men?' asked Jimmy, pacing up and down the room. 'Anything, I mean, against them?'

'No; not a single thing,' she answered. 'They were too clever. I couldn't find a single document that wasn't completely innocent.'

'I've known for a long time that there was an organised group operating and carrying on blackmail on a large scale,' he said, 'and I've suspected that these men were part of it. In the case of Webb we proved it. Papers and documents were found that proved it conclusively. What you've told me about Drake goes further to confirm my suspicions. 'Birds of a feather flock together' is an old saying, but a true one. And it applies particularly to crooks. There's somebody, too, who acts as the head of the bunch, somebody who remains in the background and who, I believe, is unknown to the others. There was a letter among Webb's effects which put this idea into my mind.'

She looked at him with quickened interest.

'Who?' she asked.

He shook his head.

'I've no notion,' he replied. 'The letter was unsigned.'

'Would it be possible,' she said, 'for this mysterious person to have been responsible for the murder of Leonard Drake?'

'There's nothing against such a theory,' he answered. 'But how is it possible to find out? We don't know the man and, after what happened at Horsham, he'll probably break up the organisation and fade into oblivion.'

'Unless Bellman can be persuaded to talk,' suggested the Angel, 'or Hathaway.'

'Bellman may quite possibly die without recovering consciousness,' said Jimmy. 'Hathaway won't say anything and neither will Leeming. Why should they? If they squeal, it'll mean long sentences for both of 'em, and if they keep quiet there's no evidence.'

'There must be evidence somewhere,' said the Angel. 'There must documents and things relating to their blackmailing activities — there must be!'

'Of course there must be,' said Jimmy. 'But where? Probably in a safe deposit or a bank, but we've no means of finding out. We can't search every safe and every bank.'

The Angel sighed and mechanically poured herself a fresh cup of coffee.

'It looks rather hopeless,' she said.

'It is hopeless and it's going to be worse,' declared Jimmy savagely. 'I don't care a darn about anything except getting you out of the mess you're in, and it's a serious one. You've broken half the laws in Christendom and, unless I can prevent it, it's all coming out at that infernal inquest.'

'I've told you not to worry about me,' she said.

'But I do worry about you!' stormed Jimmy. 'I'm only worrying about you! Darn it, woman, how can I marry you if you're in prison?'

'Oh!' The Angel was startled at his vehemence. 'I didn't know you contemplated anything of the sort,' she said feebly.

'Well, you know now,' said Jimmy crossly.

'And you may as well know that I have no intention of marrying you in prison or out of it!' she replied.

'Why?' he demanded curtly.

'Why?' she repeated. 'Well, because I — because I don't want to.'

'That seems to be a reasonable answer,' he admitted. 'Anyway I'm going to marry you, and that's that!'

'The daughter of a convicted murderer,' she said quietly. 'Don't be a fool, Jimmy! It would ruin your career.'

'If that's all you've got against it,' he retorted, 'it doesn't come into the matter at all. I sent in my resignation yesterday.'

'What?' She stared at him.

'I sent in my resignation yesterday,' he repeated doggedly. 'It doesn't take effect until the end of the month, but from then onwards I propose to live the life of a gentleman of leisure, devoting all my time to my wife and family — Who the dickens is that?'

A thunderous knocking on the front door had broken into his speech.

'I don't know — I'm not expecting anybody,' said the Angel, and then as a loud voice reached her ears: 'It's Mr. Babbington!'

Mr. Babbington it was. He came into the sitting room like a young cyclone, brushing aside Cordelia's efforts at announcing him.

'Hello-ello!' he greeted, his big face one expansive grin. 'I've been to your flat, James, and Limpet told me I should find you here, and here I am, old boy!'

'And then what?' demanded Jimmy.

'Listen, while I tell you — I've solved the secret of Uncle Ebenezer!'

'You never have!' cried Jimmy.

'I have, old boy,' said the Hon. Freddie, nodding his head vigorously. 'I have, old boy. Quite accidentally, I may say, but nevertheless a true bill for all that.'

'Well, don't make a song and dance about it,' broke in Jimmy impatiently. 'Tell us what it is — or show us.'

'Yes, do, Mr. Babbington,' said the Angel. 'You don't know how curious I am to know.'

'Lady,' said the irrepressible Freddie,

with a bow, 'thy word is law. Well, the fact of the matter is this. I had that photograph in the pocket of my jacket when we came down to Horsham. You remember, James, I was looking at it when — '

'Yes, yes, I remember all that,' interrupted his friend. 'For Heaven's sake cut the cackle and come to the horses!'

'Hang it!' said Freddie. 'Give a chap a chance! I must explain, old boy. This morning my man was looking after my clothes while I was in the bath and found Uncle Ebenezer. It's not the kind of photograph he's used to finding in my pockets, and it must have given him rather a shock. Anyhow, he brought it into the bathroom and asked what he should do with it. I told him to put it down; it was a most important relic. He did so and after I'd dried myself, I had a look at dear old Uncle Ebenezer, thinking there was something to be said for all those whiskers after all; less face to shave, you know, and all that — '

'If you don't come to the point,' threatened Jimmy, 'I shall hit you — hard!'

'Just coming to it, old boy,' said

Freddie. 'No good getting violent. Well, I was looking at the photograph when it slipped out of my hand and fell smack into the bath!'

He paused dramatically, but neither spoke.

'I fished it out as quickly as I could,' he went on, 'and mopped it with a towel and it wasn't much the worse, and then I saw that one corner had peeled away from the mount and, would you believe it, Uncle Ebenezer was not the only pebble on the beach. There was another photograph exactly the same size and everything underneath. To cut a long story short I got some clean water and peeled off Uncle Ebenezer and there was the other — not a period piece at all, old boy but the enlargement of a modern snap — and a very queer picture it is. Look here!'

He plunged a hand into his breast pocket, produced an envelope and from it a rather limp piece of cardboard.

'There, look at that, old boy,' he cried triumphantly, 'and say if little Freddie isn't the cat's boudoir slippers!'

He laid the photograph down face

upwards on the table and they bent over it. It was the picture of a piece of parkland, and in the foreground were two men. One, clearly recognisable, was pointing a revolver at the other, who was staggering back, his hands clasped to his breast. There was a cloud of smoke, and the photograph had obviously been taken at the moment when the man with the pistol had pressed the trigger.

'Bellman!' cried Jimmy. 'Bellman! And the other man's Leonard Drake — '

'Look out, old boy!' exclaimed the Hon. Freddie, and Jimmy was just in time to catch the Angel as she fell.

36

Collecting the Pieces

Jimmy Holland sat in the Assistant Commissioner's office at New Scotland Yard three days later and faced the dapper Colonel Blair across his big desk.

'We shall be sorry to lose you, Holland,' said the Assistant Commissioner. 'But you'll certainly be departing in a blaze of glory. The whole thing's amazing, but you've proved your theory about the 'Black Ring'. I must confess I was a bit sceptical.'

'I know you were, sir,' said Jimmy. 'But I was always convinced that there was something of the sort in existence.'

'Well, of course, the confession of Bellman clinches the matter. It's a thousand pities he didn't live to stand his trial for the murder of Webb.'

'It is, and it isn't, sir,' said Jimmy. 'Personally, I think it's better as it is.

We've got his confession, that's the main thing.'

'Maybe you're right.' Colonel Blair was in an agreeable mood. 'It'll be better for the girl. It would have meant a lot of unpleasant publicity for her. She was quite wrong, of course, in the attitude she adopted, but I must say I admire her pluck. By Gad! To think after all this the truth should come out. I knew Easthanger — a damned nice man — but I always thought he was guilty of shooting Drake.'

'So did everybody, sir, except his wife and his daughter and his chauffeur,' said Jimmy grimly, 'and they were right. Lord Easthanger was hanged for a crime he didn't commit.'

'The evidence was overwhelming, motive, opportunity, his own pistol, everything — Oh, well, it's no use going over all that. His memory will be cleared, that's all we can do. It was a terrible miscarriage of justice, but nobody was to blame. Bellman killed Drake because Drake discovered that he had perpetrated a fraud in his business and was blackmailing him. Dog eating dog with a vengeance.'

'And staged the crime so that suspicion was bound to fall on Lord Easthanger,' said Jimmy. 'Unfortunately for Bellman, Montgomery Webb accompanied Drake to the appointment with Easthanger, and at Drake's request concealed himself in some bushes so that Easthanger should only think he had to deal with Drake. He took a perfect picture of the murder and proceeded to do a little blackmail on his own account. A nice bunch.'

'Well, he got his deserts,' grunted Colonel Blair. 'Bellman put a stop to his blackmail when he killed him. It was lucky he dropped that photograph, though. I doubt if he would have confessed if you hadn't confronted him with that.'

'I don't think he would, sir,' agreed Jimmy. 'He tried his best to get it back.'

'What I don't quite understand,' said Blair, frowning, 'is why he locked that door at Horsham. Did he want his three friends to be burned to death?'

'Yes,' answered Jimmy. 'He wanted all the money in the 'Black Ring' for himself, and he saw a chance to get it. He was the unknown head who sent them their instructions and planned all this. They didn't know he was, because he sent letters to himself as well. All the papers and documents relating to the 'Black' business were kept in a fictitious name in a safe at the Fetter Lane deposit. The money that they squeezed from their victims was also deposited there, in cash, and shared out every month — two-thirds between the active members of the group and one-third to the 'unknown' head. This latter was sent to an accommodation address, which was different every time. Bellman appointed himself 'treasurer'. He was the only person who went to the deposit on his own instructions through the mythical head.'

'He seems to have gone to the deuce of a lot of trouble for nothing,' said the Assistant Commissioner.

'It wasn't for nothing,' said Jimmy quickly. 'It was a very cunning idea. If anything went wrong he couldn't be touched. They wouldn't squeal if they were arrested because they didn't know who he was. And he was always in close touch with them in his own capacity to see that his instructions were carried out. This happened in the case of the Angel when they abducted her from the restaurant. He couldn't interfere at the time because he was as much concerned as the others, but while she had that photograph he couldn't allow the plan that Scarthright had suggested to be carried through to its conclusion. So he 'rescued' her. In my opinion Bellman was the cleverest of the whole bunch.'

'Well, there won't be any bunch now,' said Colonel Blair. 'Bellman, Scarthright, and Phelps are dead, and Hathaway and Leeming will get seven years, I should think, so the 'Black Ring' ceases to exist.'

'And so does Detective-Inspector Holland,' said Jimmy. 'From the thirty-first of this month.'

'The first is an asset,' replied Colonel Blair. 'The second almost a national calamity!'

★ ★ ★

Three months later the boat train drew into Victoria Station and began to eject its passengers on to the long platform. Jimmy Holland, bronzed and a little broader, turned and helped his wife to alight.

'Can you see Limpet anywhere?' he said, looking along the crowded platform. 'I wired for him to meet us with the car.'

The Angel glanced quickly about.

'No, I can't,' she said. 'But I shouldn't think — Oh, there's Cordelia! Look over there!'

Jimmy followed the direction of her eyes and saw the maid walking quickly towards them. The Angel waved and Cordelia hurried up.

'I was really beginning to get afraid you'd missed the train,' she said in ultra affected drawl. 'I do 'ope you had fine weather and a desirable passage, madam.'

The Angel gasped.

'My husband is with the car,' went on Cordelia. 'An unfortunate argument between the chauffeur and a taxi-driver detained him — Oh, 'ere — ahem — here he comes now!'

The dignified and benevolent figure of Limpet was approaching rapidly.

'Your husband!' said Jimmy.

'Yes, we decided to get married soon after you left on your honeymoon sir,' answered the metamorphosed Cordelia. 'I trust that it will make no difference to our continuing to serve you in our various capacities?'

'Limpet!' breathed the aghast Jimmy. 'Limpet all over again in female form.'

'I'm sure it will make no difference at all, Cordelia,' said the Angel, her mouth twitching as she strove to check the laughter which the maid's newly-acquired accent brought bubbling up within her.

'Look here, what have you done to Cordelia?' demanded Jimmy as he and Limpet followed the luggage to the waiting car.

'In what way, sir?' inquired that dignified man.

'In her speech. She used to sound quite human — '

'I have endeavoured to instil into her some rudiments of grammar,' answered Limpet, 'and a less nasal method of articulation. I am satisfied to find such a big improvement. I occupied the greater part of our honeymoon in teaching Mrs. Limpet the correct usage of certain adjectives and a more refined method of constructing sentences. I may say that I found her an apt pupil.'

'It must have been nice for her,' remarked Jimmy dryly.

When they reached the car they found Ginger resplendent in a new uniform at the wheel and learned that old Harker was quite well. He was still running the garage, which the Angel had given him now that she had no further use for it.

'Well,' said Jimmy when the luggage had been piled on a taxi and Limpet and Cordelia had driven off with it. 'Here we are, home again. Respectable married people with leisure to enjoy life. Get in, wench and let us drive to our ancestral home!'

★   ★   ★

The sunset was almost come and the slanting light fell mellow over the churchyard at Camberley. The girl with the big bunch of crimson roses stooped and laid them gently on the grave with the little white cross. 'Sacred to the memory of Mary, Lady Easthanger — ' The inscription was new and showed clearly against the weathered stone. For a little while the girl stayed, touched by the last ray of the dying sun, and then she turned away and walked back to the man who awaited her in the car by the lychgate.

THE END

We do hope that you have enjoyed reading this large print book.

Did you know that all of our titles are available for purchase?

We publish a wide range of high quality large print books including:
Romances, Mysteries, Classics
General Fiction
Non Fiction and Westerns

Special interest titles available in large print are:
The Little Oxford Dictionary
Music Book, Song Book
Hymn Book, Service Book

Also available from us courtesy of Oxford University Press:
Young Readers' Dictionary
(large print edition)
Young Readers' Thesaurus
(large print edition)

For further information or a free brochure, please contact us at:
Ulverscroft Large Print Books Ltd.,
The Green, Bradgate Road, Anstey,
Leicester, LE7 7FU, England.
Tel: (00 44) **0116 236 4325**
Fax: (00 44) **0116 234 0205**

TERROR LOVE

Norman Lazenby

Married to Gilbert Brand, Kathryn imagines her marriage to be a happy one. It's studded with the parties of her husband's rich, socialite friends. But their attendance at a party given by his business associate, Victor Milo, tarnishes Brand's suave image. Kathryn discovers Brand attempting to strangle another guest, the nightclub singer Claudia, who becomes Kathryn's bitterest enemy. Then her world begins to crumble as she learns that Brand is an unscrupulous criminal . . . and she begins a descent into terror.

THE MING VASE

E. C. Tubb

Inside Cartwright House, a secret Government military project takes place. Men and women are well cared for, with every leisure facility. But they are prisoners, forbidden to leave. Their defection to, or capture by, foreign powers could be catastrophic. These people have very special powers, capable of being harnessed by enemies who could threaten and destroy western civilization. So when Klieger does escape, Special C.I.A. agent Don Gregson must find him. The only clue? Klieger has stolen a Ming Vase.